The Switch

Aleena Qureshi

ISBN 978-93-52013-57-9
Copyright © Aleena Qureshi, 2015

First published in India 2015 by Frog Books
An imprint of Leadstart Publishing Pvt Ltd
1 Level, Trade Centre
Bandra Kurla Complex
Bandra (East) Mumbai 400 051 India
Telephone: +91-22-40700804
Fax: +91-22-40700800
Email: info@leadstartcorp.com
www.leadstartcorp.com / www.frogbooks.net

Sales Office:
Unit No.25/26, Building No.A/1,
Near Wadala RTO,
Wadala (East), Mumbai – 400037 India
Phone: +91 22 24046887

US Office:
Axis Corp, 7845 E Oakbrook Circle
Madison, WI 53717 USA

All rights reserved. No part of this publication may be reproduced, stored in or introduced into a retrieval system, or transmitted, in any form, or by any means (electronic, mechanical, photocopying, recording or otherwise) without the prior written permission of the publisher. Any person who does any unauthorised act in relation to this publication may be liable to criminal prosecution and civil claims for damages.

Disclaimer: The Views expressed in this book are those of the Author and do not pertain to be held by the Publisher.

Editor: Joan Rodrigues
Design Editor: Mishta Roy
Layout: Chandravadan R. Shiroorkar

Typeset in Palatino Linotype
Printed at Dhote Offset Technokrafts Pvt. Ltd., Mumbai

Dedication

To my family and my readers

About the Author

Aleena Qureshi is a 20-year old student of Bachelors of Arts, with majors in English. She resides with her family in Mumbai and is passionate about writing for change. The Switch is her debut novel attempting to inspire the youth through a captivating fiction.

Acknowledgements

To all those who have made this possible.

To Leadstart my esteemed publishing house for recognising my talent and having faith in me and my story. To Malini Nair for her assistance throughout the publishing process.

To my father, Farooq Ali Qureshi for initiating the thought of writing a novel and sharing his experiences throughout. My mother, Kaneez Sughra, for her undying support and confidence in me.

My siblings Omar Qureshi, Atiya Qureshi and Zoya Qureshi for their sleepless nights in a sincere effort to move the story forward.

My editor Joan O'Brien for perfecting my language and story throughout the book.

To Kaykasshan Patel, Mustanshir Gandhi, Rohan Bhatia, Niomi Vakil, Srujani Shrawne, Jalaj Malhotra, Yash Mehta, Rohin Gupta, Jayati Kapoor, Vilomi Shah, Rutuja Veera, Aditya Shah, Abbas Lolliwala, Deeksha Dolani, Karan Gulati, Anirudh Punjabi, Ilisha Tanna, Hemant Shivdasani and Shabnam Khan for their advice and inputs for the book and it's publishing.

Thank you all very much!

Chapter 1

Lavish Life Interrupted

My coco Chanel red rouge lambskin mini classic was nowhere to be found. My heart skipped a beat. I demanded immediate attention of all my house help in its hunt.

Running through my 100-year-old multi-storey, located in Mumbai's posh Malabar hill, I realized some chaos in the living area.

"Go back to your room Aria", yelled my mother at the highest pitch of her vocal cord.

I saw my father after months and realized their problems were still not sorted. The luxurious life that was given to me by the lineage of the Oberios made me indifferent towards the undefined unexplainable problems between my parents.

Lying over my much loved round bed with a fur quilt, I began to feel its softness through my cheeks when suddenly my help, Aunt Sara, blabbered and took over the horrid mess in my room. While clearing the disastrous havoc she told me that the increased problems between my parents shouldn't affect me and I should go visit my father where he stayed. Aunt Sara was more than a help – a member of my family.

She was a healthy Christian woman in her forties and took care of me like my parents would do. She wore mid-length dresses that looked like what nurses would wear if they were allowed colours and always had a bow stuck on her dress at the waist line. She was loud and occasionally very dominating. She also informed me how the lawyers were discussing the in-depth valuation of the finances in my mother's name. I wasn't too bothered as my mind was in a conflict between the gold Versace dress and the black Dolce Gabbana that I had to wear for Westwood International's prom day. Whatever I chose, I knew there were no guesses about the prom queen.

The sweet sound of the wind chime falling on my eardrums grabbed my attention through the window to the beauty of the mesmerizing city of Mumbai. The 37 degree on a slow March day had me sinfully indulge in Baskin's malted chocolate fudge while I waited for my best friend Kiara to arrive.

I had a pretty lavish life; basically got everything I lay my finger on. Lived in Mumbai's most elite society, had amazing parents, minus their occasional problems that recently lasted more than it should have, was schooled in Ecole for sixteen years and was now part of Westwood –The junior college in Mumbai that changed my life completely in the course of two years.

Westwood International was one of the most exorbitant and staunch educational institutions located in the heart of the city. Only children of high caliber were admitted to Westwood. Once school was over every student aimed to go to Westwood. Either their scores had to be great or their parent's pockets had to be filled in order for a student to get into Westwood. It was the dream college that shaped five years of every student's life – academically, socially, morally and mentally!

Students of Westwood were unwillingly delegated into various categories, by the students' of course. I didn't give it much thought as it didn't affect me. The rich, wealthy and the most appealing were categorized as the cool and happening; everyone wanted to belong to this group. Another category was the mediocre. These tried to move upward and fit in the top. The so-called 'unfit' group was occupied by the middle class and nerds and obese and the displeasing students.

Money always created a divide and it was evident all around, but I followed my heart. I did not possess defined values at the age of 18 but I always differentiated right from wrong. On the contrary even though morals were framed into my mind by my mother since I was a kid, I always thought of life as fun, passion, adventure and thrill.

Prom was a night highly anticipated by every student since school. Every girl would put on her best attire and every guy would walk through this glamorous night with the girl he loved.

Kiara and I began getting ready. It was extremely interesting how I would curl my mid length straight tresses for every occasion while Kiara straightened her short soft curls. The grass was always greener on the other side. Nevertheless I loved everything else about myself; hazel brown eyes and fair skin were on top of the list. My model like figure, minus the tummy that bulged when I ate too much, and a height of 5.7 gave me the added advantage that most girls didn't have. If you looked too closely, which I hoped no one did, I had a very interesting birthmark on the back of the shoulder in *paan* shape. It wasn't very visible and make-up always helped cover it on special days.

As Kiara and me opened the doors of this night we had all eyes glued on how the two most edgy girls would come to junior college prom as stags, but that was us, being different and taking pride in it.

It was in those yellow lights that I realized she put extra blush on her already popping out cheek bones making her sharp eyes look smaller than usual. She had a thin and long face with a small jet black mole on the upper lip close to the nose.

The college's main hall was named D-hall due to its shape and tonight it looked massive and crazy. Students were dancing away at every corner. The entire hall was decorated with red flowers, heart-shaped balloons and other prom stickers.

Flashy lights, divulging loud music and the pitch dark of the night took every individual into a world they craved for. *What most of us today don't realize is how to come of this darkness.* This wonderful night was filled with dances, performances, food and alcohol that took over every person – some a little less, some a little more.

World no.13 and the most popular among Mumbai's youth, DJ Garry with black Sennheiser headphones on his head and hands moving swiftly over the disc, played the most grooving music that the audience spun over through the night. The bartenders had not a minute to breathe. One after another *glasses were being filled, liquids were being mixed and minds being still.* Having drunk people around me always made me feel absurd but dancing to loud music gave me happiness. Parties were always fun for me but I was always cautious as alcohol was a sin for me. All my friends would always reasonably differ.

Kiara and me sat tilted towards the bar, and spoke in length about how we planned the after-prom slumber party at my exotic mansion when suddenly something hit my foot right through my five and a half inch stilettos. I couldn't help ignore it because of the darkness. I turned around to see Kiara bend down almost touching her feet. She took out her head from her jet black straight hair and yelled, "Something's on my foot." Suddenly the dim lights in the hall faded away and we lost complete vision. The entire crowd started lifting their feet, not to the sound of music, but to the toy keyed insects that crept through their feet. My conscience kept asking if this was humour or annoyance. Who could have answered that except Rehaan? The man behind every prank in junior college. I didn't have much to say as his unprofessional act of humour proved to be amusing to the public. Having a prankster in our group was always an advantage. Rehaan, 5.7 feet tall, football fanatic with golden brown hair, round face and milk white skin colour, was the most laid back, relaxed and caring person I had ever come across. His chubby cheeks, teddy bear innocent looks made it hard for anyone to be angry with him for long. All the girls in college would eye him, but he always blushed with the attention. He hated attending lectures and would never let us attend either. So by the end of junior college all our attendances had been from 10 to 30 per cent.

When the worries of the crowd evolved into laughter, Rehaan addressed the crowd about how he practiced the less dangerous act of insects rather than the ones for which he carried a fake gun that was lying in his car. The crowd giggled.

Kaira's cell phone rang. Jay and Rahil, the other two members of our group, called her out. She hesitated to leave me alone but I assured her I would be fine. I climbed up two stairs to use the washroom and besides me was a girl half bent on the washbasin glaring at her face in the mirror. Her eyes were puffy and sore. I extended a look of pity towards her and realized I had seen her before at various parties, sitting at the bar and drinking. I could not neglect watching her beautiful face beneath the concealer hiding her dark circles. I knew of such people who ruined their lives with continuous consumption of alcohol even at such a tender age. But then who was I judging. Everyone I knew was the same. Drinking was the hype of the society. An essential part of fitting in. A social must and an image booster. Some people drank on occasions, some drank to kill the pain and some drank with no justification.

Something about her face told me she wanted help. As I walked her out of the washroom to talk to her, I heard a terrifying loud noise that gave me chills through my spine. Tripping through the stairs I thought this was the last piece of sound that fell on my eardrums. I could not get myself to explain the reason behind this intimidating loud noise.

In the next two minutes I stood still between a human stampede. Everybody ran aimlessly from one corner to another not knowing where they were headed. The commotion made me move in the opposite direction of the sound. This uproar was apparently caused by a nighthawk pistol that was shot in the air leaving a bullet hole in the pretty decorated ceiling next to a preciously heavy chandelier. My eyes rolled down to the person holding the gun. Dressed in black from head to toe, the person resembled exactly what Bollywood movies portrayed thieves to be. The first gunshot created a humungous chaos in which most of the students eloped from the various exits in the hall. The chief guests, DJ, security – all ran for their lives. I could see the door wide open right in front of me but I couldn't get myself to walk out of it without Rehaan. I knew for a matter of fact that he did not leave the place. For the two years that I knew him he always put his friends before himself. He would never leave the place leaving behind others in danger. Soon another bullet was released from the gun of another criminal dressed exactly the same. He screamed for everyone's attention and demanded their hands to be in the air. Amidst all of this my head spun right to left looking for Rehaan and I was suddenly pushed to the floor, flat on my face. Blood excruciated from my nose and my temperament rose. I shrieked like a werewolf looking at the moon in the sky when I was pulled back from my waist in the most inhuman manner having my mouth taped. The one devil now turned into three, hostaging thirty-five students and two teachers of the city's most reputed college.

The black men, as I would like to call them, whispered something to each other and then blatantly pointed their guns towards us. I instantly sensed a feeling of profound fear and racing heartbeat. They made us sit down on the floor and one of them collected all our cell phones and dumped them into a huge cardboard box. Looking closely at the hands with the gun I could see a trembling closed fist. It cleared at least one answer off my mind – these weren't professional shooters. They called each other by numbers so no one knew of their identity. The mask that they wore focused their attention on the only part of their body that was revealed, their eyes. Thousands of thoughts and various questions kept flashing my mind. What were they doing here? What did they want? Who were they? And why were a bunch of high school children their prime targets?

We keep asking ourselves a million questions throughout the course of our lives, some are answered, some we are always searching for and some find places in our graves...but throughout the course of our lives we should know that some answers are to be known, some answers are to be searched for and some are best taken to the grave.

One of them signalled the other to untape me and the first thing that came out of my mouth was "what do you want?" As angry as I looked asking this, the more unnerved I was to listen to the black man's response. "To make you realize", he dragged his words and scared me with awfully red wide-open eyes when the other one clapped his hand to hint him to not talk. I quietly sat down regretting my words that could have initiated a more violent response that would prove to be harmful for everyone in the room. While they mumbled to each other, my mind crossed over how a dazzling night turned into a nightmare. Thirty minutes ago this massive hall was full of energy and life and now we were succumbed to pressure and fear of the unpredictable happenings of the night. The feeling of a tragic event had filled our hearts with silence. Tears rolled down cheeks, fingers came together, necks bent down and fear dominated over all the faces. The black men kept hovering above our heads as bees on a hive. The two teachers tried consoling the students by constantly giving them hope that things would be fine.

"Hey Aria", said a soft shrill voice from a girl beside me with tears in her eyes.

"My name is Tanya".

"I can't seem to place you", I said.

She told me that she wanted my coat as she was cold. I immediately gave it to her. I asked her how she knew my name and she said that everyone knew me.

She added soberly, "Everyone knows the first category but you wouldn't even know we are in the same English class because I don't belong to the same social class as you".

I took my eyes away from her and looked down; I was spellbound and too taken aback to even answer her. I felt a certain pinch in my heart and I asked myself if I was really that indifferent to everyone other than my group of friends. I was sorry but I couldn't help it. That was the way society was. I couldn't be best friends with just about anybody. We had standards to maintain and a certain type of people to hang out with.

I could hear the seconds' hand moving across the huge wall clock. My contact lenses itched, my make up was wearing off but what I was most irritated about was how my Versace dress was sweeping through the dirty floor as I moved. I didn't understand how these few men could have the nerve to try and hurt or kill students who were children of the city's biggest names coming from the most influential backgrounds. What do they think of themselves? How could they even think of doing something like that to me or my friends and think of easily getting away? I know that my father would not leave these men.

I began to rub my hands together to keep myself warm when a sudden beep from inside my bag startled me. I realized then that my BlackBerry Bold 4 was taken away but my iPhone was still in my bag. I looked around and waited for their attention to be elsewhere but that didn't seem to be happening. I cautiously acted as if I was removing a handkerchief from my bag and unlocked my phone inside it."come 2 d loo near d fire exit asap", was a WhatsApp message from Rehaan. I hated how he would use those short forms that made it harder to read what was written.

Without a moment's thought I stood up on my feet acting as if my bladders were bursting. Number three told number one to go right to the door with me. I told him to keep his tacky hands off me, to which he was obviously very offended. I twisted the knob of the door and turned around giving him a nasty look that inferred, now are you going to come in? I locked the door behind me and saw Rehaan standing at the other end of the ladies washroom with his eyes glued to the phone. His face never incorporated his feelings. I ran towards him with long footsteps and hugged him like it took off all worries. I wrapped my arms around his waist and dug my face into his chest. His extreme strong smell added to my closeness and relief. *Just looking at people that matter to you the most in times of need can change the way you feel about a situation.* I felt safer but we had no time. He had already informed the police and they were on their way. He took my phone and called Rahil's father. His father was the home minister of Mumbai and a highly responsible man of power and authority. We came to know that his father already knew about the situation as Rahil called him earlier to tell him that the students were all being taken to jail for their statements and would be left only after a parent came and signed them off.

While his dad said that he was on his way we heard the washroom door being banged on. Before we could begin to think, the horrid man came in pointing his revolver at us. Our reflexes made our hands go up in the air dropping our phones on the slippery beige marble flooring. He came running towards us with full force and hit Rehaan hard on his calves, knocked him down and kept him on his knees. I quickly grabbed the glass vase kept near the washbasin and aimed it hard on his head. He fell on top of Rehaan causing Rehaan's sudden astonishment. He knew that I had never tried killing an insect before in my life.

He held my hand and we rushed to figure out how to leave but while we were trying to sneak out one devil came from behind and caught Rehaan's hand as tightly as he could. The other one went to the washroom and while helping the bruised man, seized our phones. He called the last dialled number on my phone and his next few words took me by shock "I will leave all the students if you let me take Aria with me. She will be back soon safe and sound. If not everyone will suffer!

Once again a million obvious questions over powered my mind like the math equations of 10th grade that I could never solve. But Rehaan was more furious.

I yelled furiously "You're not getting anything you understand, just go away or you pay".

I kept looking at Rehaan as though everything else in the room was still. I felt two seconds of an astonished loving feeling. Saying something revengeful at this time would definitely risk his life, but he did not think twice for my sake.

They say though times test us, and in situations like these when someone gives us all they have, it makes us believe that we are not alone; someone out there is always going to be with us. It ultimately makes us a stronger person with faith, belief and higher self-confidence. Such people impact our lives for good and we should learn to never let them go.

My respect for his friendship ascended and when I came back from the stillness I realized I was being taped, again. We all sat there again, sulking quietly, wishing this never took place and what we could do to bring ourselves out of this problem. Some strange vague noises of chattering and thumping feet grew louder by the minute and gave me a slight ray of hope just when I was praying to God. Minutes later we heard Rahil's father speak. A powerful and heavy voice on the mike commanded, "All four sides of the school are guarded, if you do not leave the children we will be forced to come in and open fire".

The men started picking up their belongings and began to run. I assumed that they did not anticipate such a scenario. Quickly on the way one of them grabbed my hand and pulled me with them dragging me across the hall. I resisted and pushed myself away as strongly as I could. That day I understood how men are physically stronger than women.

As soon as Rehaan started following me, the number two man turned to him with his pistol pointing towards his leg and what happened next brought my heart into my mouth. His finger on the trigger, pushing it lightly towards the inside of the hole space. My eyes stared at that trigger wanting the pistol to not work. The voice had now become familiar but this time my jaws dropped in disbelief and I shrieked out loudly.

I could not believe what my eyes had just witnessed. My throat was dry and my hands were trembling and sweating. My brains could not take the trauma that just struck me. I somehow wanted the clock to reverse. Rehaan fell on the ground with his leg bleeding continuously and as much as I tried I was not let lose enough to run to him. I felt completely helpless and shattered. This was happening to him because of me. Those men wanted me then why shoot him? Anger, confusion and regret governed me. I still kept pushing hard and moving furiously in the most inhuman manner trying to get away from them.

They took me through the exit entering the hallway into the library. The end of the library had a small window that they lifted and pushed me into. This closed space was a small dirty disgusting place with the room for barely two humans to sit cross legged. The greasy dark quarter felt as though rats lived in it. It was stinking and had spider webs all around; I also saw some rag like clothing items at the extreme left end. I could not stop weeping thinking about what Rehaan must be going through. They regularly peeped into a small hole to see if the police was entering the premises. After about fifteen minutes in that terrible, suffocating place an announcement was made from outside "the police have entered the school and it would be recommended to surrender". Immediately after, they began to escape from the other window exit that led to the street. My assumption of them not anticipating that scenario was obviously incorrect. I highly doubted if anyone ever knew of this place. It was quiet evident that this place was extremely well known to these men and their entrance would have also been made from here.

Two of them had now left and the third one grabbed my hand to take me along with him. He tried to grab my hand but I had not given up yet. I tried to fight back and gave him a few punches. My delicate hands and low energy had his body unaffected by my actions. I now decided that here my anger was supposed to take direction. I had to plan to use my strength mentally and not physically. So I practiced what I was taught at a safety drive for women in my eighth grade and kicked him hard between his legs. This was easy to do as we were not very far away and my Louboutins were new and pointed. We were trying to constantly sit, bend and fold our legs in that tiny place. He now had both his hands covering his private parts and my next move was an instant reflex. My long nails spontaneously tried to get his black cloth mask off his face and as his confusion sought after what I was trying to do my filed nails had now pierced into his mask and ripped it apart. I was completely flabbergasted by what I saw next. My patience for shocks in one night had reached its peak. His fast breathing and perspiration took me aback. His face and expression thrilled me while his eyes confirmed his fear. The combination of his eyes with his nose made it hard for me to believe he was the person I knew.

An individual's life is always filled with great diversities, some with greater impact than the others. The notion always confides that when people are differentiated from each other by birth or capabilities, one is meant to suffer more than the other. The fact remains on how one takes a situation and its impact. A positive outlook to a fairly disastrous situation could lead an ease through it but a fairly negative outlook to the same situation can make it worse. When you are born into a wealthy family circumstance, you lead an easy life and mine was just so. What problems came and went were how big I made them. But when a life-turning situation as an act of capture, attempt of killing and fear of death takes place you question your strength to face difficulties. Such a hard hit situation had never taken place in my life and for the first time I was in a real and unsafe situation that made me feel vulnerable.

I ran across the library with whatever little breath I had left, sweeping the floor after the men left through the tunnel and fell on my knees panting in the hallway. I was instantly surrounded by the police and fell into the arms of my parents. I pointed my finger towards the library as I had no stamina to talk and told the squad about the small room near the science fiction section. The lines on the forehead of my parents indicated how worried and relieved they were to see me. They told me the other students were safe with their parents answering questions about these men and their motives. They got me orange flavour Glucon D for my weakness and inhaler for my minor asthma.

I was the only one who knew about one of them but decided to keep it to myself because of the fact that this entire situation was related to them having something to do with me. The cops took over the entire college for supervision and evidence.

Leaving the college premises with tired eyes and a tired mind I saw Rahil and Jay run towards me and asked me if I was fine. They told me about the situation at the station and how some students were still waiting for their parents to sign them off. They were sorry that they couldn't be with me through this and I told them that it was not in their hands. I enquired about Rehaan.

"Breach Candy hospital with Kiara", they said. The only thing that I wanted to do next was to see Rehaan. I begged my parents to let me go but they decided ardently that they would come along.

White creased bed sheets, artificial flowers, slow movement of the fan and the typical hospital room smell overpowered Rehaan's existence on the bed. His wounded leg was covered in layers of bandage dressing and he looked at my face without a blink in his eyes. He stretched a half smile to me. I ran to him and sunk my face in his arms while his hands moved swiftly caressing my forehead. Sobbing I continued telling him what had happened with me. "I know who he is. **He's the boy from our class**".

Chapter 2

An Exotic Trip and Its Effects

As hard as you try to keep, sometimes the best thing to do is to let out feelings.

He was still to my words and I told him that we would keep this between us and only think of what to do about it once everything becomes normal again.

I hated coming to hospitals, not only did the smell make me nauseous but so did looking at people suffering. The way I was bought up, I was always kept away from pain, sadness, sickness and grief; but what always kept me going was how my mom once told me that *god gives as much pain a person can stand*. I was a faithful follower of the almighty or maybe I thought so looking at other people around me with no faith at all. What shocked me more was how they thought the world works purely on science. I didn't follow any religion but always believed that there is someone who runs this universe. I never stressed on the topic as I always thought there's enough time in life to figure it out when I was older; but here in India, the more we learn things about religion the more religions we are exposed to. It does nothing but confuses us. My mom followed Hinduism, but only for the name I assumed. She believed anything any *pandit* would tell her. I would ask her if god suggested such things or if there was any logical reasoning behind them. To my surprise, she would call me disobedient. Elders had a smooth way out for being elders – always!

I could tell that Rehaan was really disturbed and in a lot of pain. His parents kept coming at regular intervals to keep a check on him. The nurses followed the same pattern. Kiara, Rahil and Jay came and stood around the bed, speechless and sad. We held each other's hands and stood by each other like we had been since the past two years.

I broke the silence, and with my speech breaking into regular chunks I told them how much they meant to me and how I never wanted to lose them.

With special permission and heavy bribes the four of us stayed back with Rehaan in the hospital with his parents in the adjacent room while our parents left for their respective houses. Our sleep had wandered places to come back to us at this unearthly hour, so we spoke in length about the incidents of the night and its impact on us. Those feelings of pain and fright had not faded away – not in any of us. The chills and tremors still ran through my blood. The anticipatory fright of what was going to happen was still prevalent through the hair-raising experiences of Jay and Rahil as they spoke.

Rahil told us what had happened outside "There was panic outside the college. Even more at the station where the parents were panicking. No one had any idea what was happening. The college authorities were questioned by the police about how inefficient their security system was. This was the best college in town and now its name would be flooded in the papers in the negative light".

"There were constant calls being made by everyone to somehow get a hold on what was happening inside. Calls were being made to tell the parents about their children and to the police or help". Rahil added "Our principal Mr Shah stood outside college with shock and amazement on how something like this could even take place. He knew his and the school's reputation was in danger".

I wanted this conversation to end. I looked around at the night sky and the smiling sea under it, calm and composed. The waves were sober; unnatural for a sea I always saw as violent. The waved kissed the shore silently in the dark every few minutes, went back in a way to tell her she would be back.

We decided to give our police report with extreme scrutiny while being questioned the next morning. Kiara suddenly threw herself on the big grey couch away from the bed.

"Remember all those times we bunked lectures and went for drives? How we made our drivers and servants sign our defaulters for college". She laughed hesitantly.

"It was hilarious" added Jay as we all laughed.

Our talks slowly sublimed into the past as we started cherishing all the fun times we had together these two years, but most importantly how it all began during the epic trip to Aamby Valley.

A dull boring day at college was revived by good news. A news that made our minds and bodies function again. Our class teacher read out a long detailed description from the three-page stapled sheets that the tallest peon, Shankar, got to her notice. He mostly always got dull and boring news with his patented straight face look and unkempt frizzy hair, about when our exams would be or how some teacher wanted us to assemble for a meeting somewhere in the college.

On 2nd February, 2010, we were to leave for a seven-day compulsory trip to Aamby Valley to explore its breath-taking beauty and take a break from our hectic curriculum. No sooner pictures of our trip had already began coming into our minds as we all passed the circular across the class. This much needed break for me was not only from my studies but also from my parents. It was weird to me that my parents were married but lived separately. I wondered when that would get over. They were very strong-headed individuals, and for most of the times, that was a major problem. They mostly had similar views, but when it differed, it would create a lot of problems.

College had only began 3 weeks back; Kiara and I had not made a lot of friends by then and most of our school friends were separated, so I thought this would be a good chance to start all over again. All I did till the 2nd of February was prepare for the entire trip. I had a new reason to shop for – got some new studs and fancy adventure sports items from Nike and Adidas. Shopping was the best therapy ever. I could shop all my life. The happiness of buying things was more than using them.

Most Mumbaikars would always go to Lonavala over the weekends as it was the nearest feasible getaway but Aamby Valley was one level up. Financially and topographically. Expensive and lavishly designed for the well-to-do. Situated in the outskirts of the city, Aamby Valley was known for its impressive facets of luxurious living, leisure and recreation. Away from the hectic life of the city, this valley was spread over more than 10000 acres of land.

Along with Kiara, Jay too studied in the same school with us, so I knew him quiet well for four years now. He was quite an extrovert like me, he always ate as though he saw food after four days and still, by no means, grew fat. He would never forget to mention that his metabolism was great. He was known for his whacky new hairstyles every now and then, and they varied from being Caesar cut to pineapple and sometimes even weird Mohawks. His nose was huge and flat in the centre. He had eyelashes as long and thick as a girl's. He was also our go-to adviser for any electronic related query. From cell phones to laptops and Windows to Android. I secretly once overheard him tell Rehaan that he wasn't better at electronics, he was just better at googling it!

In our two-hour long journey by road in groups of five, Jay and Kiara came along. The only unsaid issue I had was Jay getting his friend Rahil along. I never really spoke to Rahil and thought of him being extremely self-obsessed. His baggy jeans below his waist sweeping the floor and his collar up straight to his jaw line made me dislike him even before he opened his mouth. But it seemed like my college classified that as trendy and fashionable.

While leaving, Jiah was put in our group. She looked anorexic but still always showed off her legs wearing short shorts thinking she looked good. I wondered why people didn't look at the mirror often. The yawns through our entire journey proved our early morning itinerary to be extremely painful. We reached in the afternoon to straight jump to lunch at the Shallot's allocated to us. There was buffet for us with a vast variety of veg and non-veg dishes. We ate to our hearts content. We were then taken to Sandstone Park where the greenery had our eyes stuck to the view. The pristine and translucent water between the valley enabled us to see the vibrant colourful fishes. A slight cut mountain section had the river water flow horizontally as our eyes witnessed one of the most magnificent waterfalls ever. Our cameras did not stop clicking pictures. Another section one km away was designed for recreational activities. Tight rope walking was what I longed for. The thrill of being between two ropes without a harness in the middle of the air at a height of 25 feet was particularly exciting. We walked all over the area till our eyes were glued to the view. I was so excited about tight rope walking that I didn't wait for a single second after looking at the thick piece of rope. I began my thrilling tight rope walk before anyone could, with a lot of difficulty and yelling and giggling I reached mid-way. Behind me was Rehaan waiting for his turn, I stopped in the middle, I was tired, my arms ached, so I thought I'd rest for a few seconds, but the impatient soul that Rehaan was, he began to walk before I finished. His 75 kg weight on the thin rope made me lose my balance separating one leg from another while the rope cut my skin from the arm and thigh as I fell. Embarrassment mixed with anger had me cover my face and sit sulking in one corner watching everyone else. The pain in my spine from the fall made me think that my entire trip was ruined because of this idiot. Those thoughts slowly subsided as constant medical care was given to me.

Rehaan, who was laughing with the others while I fell, came to me with the most serious face and spoke to me for the first time in spite of being with me in the same class. I was in no mood to listen to any justifications but he ignored that fact and went ahead

"I didn't intend to hurt you, I was just having fun". He came close and looked deeply into my wound and grabbed my arm from the back and blew over it, took some cream and started applying over it. I pulled my hand back but his fingers pressed harder as he held my hand more steadily while draping it with the surgical tape. I thought to myself how dominating he was and I still gave him angry looks as he left. His finger marks stayed red on my sensitive fair skin for the next five minutes.

I sat sulking and watch everyone else do bungee jumping and mountain climbing. We then came back to our cottages and our evening was spent in the hotel relaxing. Early next morning we were taken to watch a water show that took place in Aamby every day from 8 am to 8.20 am. Nature astonished me with each day during this trip. Something I never appreciated before. A number of water spouts releasing water were presented in a manner that pleased the eyes. Water sprung right in the air and came back down again. They made shapes by twisting and twirling and radiated with their background colour. The quantity, friction, height and criss-cross of the water made it look like a piece of art, a thorough pleasure to the eyes and peace to the mind. We then went for a boat ride that gave me motion sickness as it lasted for more than half an hour while the boys took to speed boating. We proceeded to the local market later in the day to find artistic valuables, gift items, intricate food items and souvenirs to take back home.

That night was a particularly interesting one. I woke up Kiara who was snoring away right next to me. I hated it about her. I kicked her really hard most of the times when she would sleep next to me so she would get disturbed and stop snoring. But she always began again.

"Kiara wake up. Have you come here to sleep?"

She resisted waking up but I was ardent on having some fun.

"What is your problem? Let me sleep". She took out the pillow from under her head and placed it on her forehead. I dragged her out of bed as she held my shorts. I was stubborn and always got what I wanted. She didn't have an option.

We came out of our cottage and called for others. No one answered their doors. We then went to the other cottage and found Rehaan hiding and eating a burger in one corner of the two-storey shallot staircase. We both burst into a laughter riot looking at him hide and eat like a thief. Our giggling had not subsided and we went ahead to ask him if he wanted to sneak out for the night with us and he spontaneously ran before us as though it was his plan. I phoned Jay to join us and he got Rahil along. We came together like a group of robbers and started walking out on our toes making minimal noise. We reached outside the Shallot to see the watchman snoring away with his cap covering half his head and the stick motionless between his fingers. We walked two miles silently. Any word from us felt like we had mikes fixed in our throats. The echo of my voice startled me so I decided to keep it low. We then reached the middle of a jungle-looking area that was extremely dark and decided to grab woods from nearby and light a bonfire. I loved bonfires. It was the thing about fire. It was arrogant, restless and had the power to destroy when provoked.

We were pleased to find a matchbox in Rahil's pocket that he had apparently reserved for his smokes. Judgmental that I was, when I saw Rahil with a smoke in one hand and his cell phone in the other sitting in one corner away from us I presumed him to be antisocial and inconsiderate in addition to what I already thought of him. To break the ice with him I went and sat next to him and tried to make him feel comfortable so that he would open up and I would then know the reason for his different behaviour. This was typical me. I loved jumping into unnecessary situations and acting as though I was the only understanding person who could solve anything in this world. I would go up and talk to anyone as if I were their best friends and knew them forever.

I didn't look into his eyes, it would make it weird; so I looked around pretending to admire the dark and abruptly asked him why he liked staying aloof and resisted making friends. He turned his head towards me, looked at me with glaring fearsome eyes and remained silent. Fine lines passed through my forehead and his intense look now worried me. I felt like this was a big mistake and got up without a word to move towards the bonfire.

I took two steps and heard him say, "Have you ever been left alone? Have you ever been cheated? Has someone ever broken your trust?"

As I sat down next to him he began whining about a girl, "she was pretty, she was helpful, she was my life. Until one day she went away".

How poetic, I thought in my head.

"I loved her for two years, she left me for another

guy and since then I have never trusted anyone because everyone is selfish", he added.

I was disappointed by his negative thoughts. He remained depressed even today, six months after that.

"I'm telling you this because no one has ever asked me why I keep away. Everyone thinks I have an attitude but I don't care because *it's better to be with less and true people around than more and fake"*, he believed.

After carefully scrutinizing his words, I told him "You don't have to be so negative and one bad relationship does not define people as a whole".

He sighed and stubbed his cigarette not believing my words. By looking at his gloomy face I thought it would be best to change the topic and so I took out my pink Sony camera to randomly take pictures of my friends sitting away at the bonfire when I suddenly heard a startling clear noise of three loud claps from the woods behind us. My instant reflex had me cling to Rahil due to the daunting fear of something abnormal. His reaction told me that I was not the only one to hear that dreadful noise.

We quickly ran to the bonfire and I begged for all of us to go back to our Shallots. None of them believed what we saw and thought we were joking but agreed to go back. Quietly walking back from the woods I was freaked out at everything that came in front of me, from tiny insects to the branches of the trees. I decided to avoid them and began to sing "I walk a lonely road" in the middle of the street. All of us decided to stay together at the cottage allotted to Rehaan and two other friends of his. The eerie sound of the opening of the door made my heart beat faster. We switched on the lights to find our spots to sleep in. As I moved a pillow off its place from the bed I saw the sheets under it covered in stains of blood. I shrieked instantly and jumped away from my place. Rahil, Jay and Rehaan were quick to come and stand next to me while Kiara hid her face under her blanket and screamed loudly. Rehaan and Jay's trembling hands took me away from the place as Rahil demanded that we call for help. Rehaan then lifted the sheets and folded them over keeping them aside.

A supernatural incident does not come easy, but when it does it hits hard. A series of questions of reality run through our practicality-fed minds, and our failure to link the two results in utter confusion. We want to believe that the world works on science and that is what we are always taught but earth governs more than what science can teach.

We had no idea what was going on around us but we knew that all we could do at this time was to run or get help. Rehaan and I went to the room where Ryan and Kunal were sleeping and woke them up immediately. As Kunal sat halfway through we saw a thin red streak on his upper lip. He ran his finger in circular motion and was amazed to see the vision. His nose was bleeding continuously for no valid reason. We ran down with both of them screaming in fright. We then stood in line one behind the other and started leaving the place. As I stood at the door trying to get out, the bathroom door at a distance behind us shut on its own and latched itself. I turned around. I was numb to see the scene till Rehaan pulled me from my place and took me out of the chalet. There was no one near the bathroom door neither was there any wind around.

We all ran to our school staff's chalet. Four members of the faculty snoring away in the chalet woke up shocked to see the five of us panting and telling our stories in the middle of their sound sleep. We were then kept in the chalet being consoled the whole night. Our teachers decided they would go check things out properly the next morning with some local residents. We were made to sleep in there congested along with our teachers. The four male teachers slept upstairs. They were too woken up and enlightened. Their anger about us sneaking out of our chalet at night was clear on their faces and we knew we were in deep trouble.

Early next morning the locals of Aamby Valley were inquired about the history of such events. They were then taken to the chalet and extreme scrutiny was done investigating the place. When asked how we changed chalets and reached there, we told them about our little adventure in the woods. All our teachers looked at us as raw meat while we all looked down in embarrassment. They took the five of us back to the same place again in daylight and asked us what we did there.

"We made a bonfire here ma'am", Rehaan told Mrs. Tandon.

Rahil, Jay and Kiara gave them long details while I slowly took Rehaan in one corner and whispered to him "Should we tell them about the alcohol that the other three were having?"

"The consequences would be horrible but if we want to stay here for three more nights safely then we ought to inform them I think".

"I think so too". I thought stressfully.

We convinced the three of them to confess and they agreed.

We walked ahead in small steps, stood between our teachers and took the courage to tell them turn by turn. Their faces turned red with rage and their yelling voices began to rotate in my head like hammer on nails. The most shocking reaction came from a local resident whose hands covered his mouth as though we announced someone's death.

He began to tell us that the land in the woods was ominous. The area behind, deeper in the woods, was occupied by dead people…it was a graveyard. They then continued to specify that supernatural incidents have taken place there before and all local residents believe that if the existence of a soul on that land is disturbed in any form, they become active and may retaliate in some manner. Kiara and Rahil began to laugh loudly while Rehaan was quiet. I, on the other hand, with total seriousness completely believed everything that he said.

"Are you crazy?" said Rahil "There has to be a logical explanation to the things happening in the woods, you guys live in the 18th century, this cannot be true".

"I agree, let's go from here", added Kiara.

The teachers then took a collective decision to leave that side of the river in Aamby Valley for the rest of the stay.

Paranormal and supernatural incidents can be defined as outside the range of normal, not subject to the nature of law. The lack of physical and scientific explanations to such incidents makes it difficult to assess a situation with concrete conclusions. We may or may not believe certain illogical experiences of people but those in it perceive a sense of reason for these traumatic, sometimes life-changing events and its impact on human life.

That night we somehow managed to gain our share of sleep and early next morning decided to sit by the pool under the morning sun.

The sky was host to the glistening sun and a few smoky looking vague blue clouds. Tall coconut trees stood around the sides of our chalets and swung around like they sang happily. We sat near the pool but it seemed like our entire batch wanted to get into one small Jacuzzi. I sat to read my Bible, the *Vogue*, on the sun-kissed grass of the lawn attached to the pool. Concentrating on what to buy next I heard some gossiping and giggling going on between Kiara, Rahil and Rehaan which I ignored without giving much importance. I was wondering how I could catch a grasshopper 3 feet away from me, whose existence bothered my living. I hated insects; they were so creepy that I wondered why they existed. The giggles soon turned louder and the sound then mixed with a huge splash of gigantic water noise. I instantly stood on my feet in utter amazement.

Jay was pushed into the water by Kiara, Rahil and Rehaan as part of their prank. Jay struggled in the water when Ryan from the other corner of the pool yelled ghastly, "Pull him out, he does not know how to swim". Without a second's thought in the shock-still surrounding, Rehaan and I jumped into the pool. We had not a moment to think. I had held my breath and jumped as close to him as I could and tried to hold him near the waist to lift and push him up but he was too heavy. The fraction of a second that the incident took place, made it hard for me to think of how else to save him, so I began trying whatever I could. Rehaan then reached the bottom of the seven feet pool and bent down and fit Jay's feet on his back and then pushed himself up against the base of the pool. Jay breathed air for a few seconds but Rehaan couldn't hold longer. By then lifeguards had reached and pushed me aside. All three of us were removed and Jay lay down still breathless. My lips only chanted prayers for him to be alright. As his chest was pressed and pushed rigorously he gained back his breath while water flowed out of his mouth. We breathed a sigh of relief. Kiara, Rehaan and Rahil were equally worried. They still could not digest the fact that Jay did not know how to swim and had not anticipated such an incident. The guilt showed effectively on their faces.

"It was entirely my fault, I had planned it." Said Rehaan, "I thought it would be fun and harmless".

Jay then answered coughing, "It's alright, I knew you'll did not have any bad intentions".

"Sorry Jay", added Kiara and Rahil together.

Chapter 3

Drama or Reality

Beep! The alarm in the hospital rang as an emergency call was made by some room on the same floor as ours. Kaira then commented on our walk down the memory lane, "Time flies so quickly, it feels like those incidents of Aamby Valley had just taken place, I can't believe it's been two years since the unforgettable trip, time really flies!!"

Jay then added as to how our friendship grew in the days of our performing arts inter-college competition. After this trip and making a few friends we decided to actively take part in college activities. I was extremely excited about the topics being Shakespeare's plays and our college opted for the epic cross star lovers' story of Romeo and Juliet.

At audition day my high-level drama skills bagged me the role of the sober Juliet. Kiara was chosen to be the assistant director to Mrs. Mary, our dramatics head. Rahil was casted as Mercutio, Romeo's best friend and Rehaan, to everyone's surprise was made Romeo.

Our rehearsals began soon enough with a vague set up of the stage and characters with all the students reading their dialogues from the manuscripts. The stage was divided into two sides showcasing the two rival families Montague and Capulet. Two hours every day was conceptualized for rehearsals. We started memorizing the dialogues of the play and slowly developed a sense of attachment to the characters we played. Interacting with Jay, however, was the most hilarious part. He played the role of count Paris, a contender to marry Juliet, and every time we spoke our dialogues looking at each other we would burst into loud chunks of laughter.

On the 15th day of our practice when we were supposed to leave the scripts at home and memorize dialogues, we began to start realizing that this wasn't a cakewalk. The balcony scene where I begin my monologue made me extremely nervous. Rehaan would always say his lines with complete sincerity. He was good with memory and way faster than me. I would take four readings of one page to memorize it while he just read it once. I peeped from a rough cardboard-made dummy window from a little above him and looked down straight into his eyes as he read his lines with perfection.

"But soft, what light through yonder window breaks?
It is the east and Juliet is the sun!
Arise, fair sun, and kill the envious moon,
Who is already sick and pale with grief
That thou her maid art far more fair than she.
Be not her maid, since she is envious;
Her vestal livery is but sick and green,

And none but fools do wear it. Cast it off.
It is my lady, O, it is my love!
O that she knew she were!
She speaks, yet she says nothing; what of that?
Her eye discourses, I will answer it.
I am too bold: 'tis not to me she speaks.
Two of the fairest stars in all the heaven,
Having some business, do entreat her eyes
To twinkle in their spheres till they return.
What if her eyes were there, they in her head?
The brightness of her cheek would shame those stars,
As daylight doth a lamp. Her eyes in heaven
Would through the airy region stream so bright
That birds would sing and think it were not night.
See how she leans her cheek upon her hand
O that I were a glove upon that hand,
That I might touch that cheek!"

I could not buy the fact that he was reading out dialogues. In my heart I felt that those words were for me. He then held me from my waist and grabbed me towards him. There was complete silence in the hall.

"Your line Aria", yelled Mrs. Mary, my eyes still glued on Rehaan.

He then took his hands back and I had forgotten every line that I was supposed to say.

"Pack up!" she said. We were done for the day.

The five of us decided to grab some yogurt from six street and play monopoly deal at home, but I was completely lost that day. I was lost in my thoughts, not knowing why I was lost. I couldn't concentrate. So while we started playing I sneaked glances at those gleaming eyes of his. I couldn't stop looking. Kiara overlooked and gave me a tap on my shoulder and hummed, "ahem ahem".

"Play your game", I said blushing.

That night I began to dream – a conflicting chain of ongoing dreams where I wondered where this feeling came from and where it would go. What meaning it had and why couldn't I explain it. I had never felt like this before. I was smiling to myself. I was thinking about him. But I needed to stop. This shouldn't go where it was going. He was my friend and I couldn't spoil that. He never thought of me like that. I should stop overthinking I told myself. I spoke to myself rather much.

Next day at rehearsals I was a different person. I was smiling and joyful all day for no reason. I kept my calm though, trying to be all normal but my heart beat faster every time he came closer. Mrs. Mary had a long day and backstage gossip told us that she was worried as she didn't have a costume designer for our play. So I instantly went to her and asked if I could design the clothes for the show. It was an abrupt idea, but that's how I was.

"You're not experienced Aria", she said sadly.

I tried to assure her saying "I do some sketching during my free time and I could show it to you, I won't let you down. I promise".

"Will you be able to manage being Juliet and doing this?"

"Of course", I said.

"Okay let me see your work and then I will tell you".

I started making new sketches for the play appropriate for the characters. I began with the main characters first. I wanted the costumes to look rich and classy and still be subtle reflecting that era. I did a little research on the Internet. When I saw my sketches after doing it a few times I tore them and made new ones. I thought it was actually easy to go and hire them from the store but this was my time to show my creativity. I went to Mrs. Mary before our practice the next day and showed her a few of my old sketches. I added two of my Shakespearian sketches too. I briefed her about how I would go about hiring a tailor and how I would make the look for each character based on the era they came from. She was highly impressed and let me go ahead with it. So my summer was busy with learning dialogues and designing clothes.

Our rehearsals gradually became more tedious as our work increased. Mrs. Mary made us do the entire play over and over again. Kiara on the other hand always let go our mistakes. I had started giving the tailor the fabric that I wanted along with directions on how to stitch it.

16th June, 2010!

Performing arts had several dynamics, from body language to hand gestures and from speech to voice intonation. It's the ability of a person to display a character different from their own and portray the feelings and concepts of that person in that environment. The most difficult part being the performance in front of an audience, an audience who will judge: whom you would have to convince your character to. Those, for whom you have to construct laughter and pain and joy and grief. Make them feel what your character feels and think how your character does.

This was my day to represent the smart, beautiful and witty Juliet in front of a very diverse audience. Audience among whom were not only my school members but also members of other school and participants. I was extremely nervous and hoped to do justice to the character and get the trophy for my school. Rehaan on the other hand was as calm as one could be. He just never worried. He laughed at how seriously I took this.

Santan Hall was filled that day; it was where all the big dramas of the city took place. Apart from being humongous, the hall was in the shape of a dome, all sides covered with thick red cloth. There were about 500 seats in the auditorium which was slowly and steadily getting filled. The stage was, however, the brightest and most vivacious. The wooden flooring like every other stage gave me the performance feeling. I kept stamping my foot at it and listening to the sound. I loved wooden flooring. It was the feel of olden days that interested me. As the place started getting occupied, my nervousness increased. Kiara and me held hands and tried to remain calm. I repeated all the dialogues in front of her that I found difficult to remember.

As time passed, the noise increased. There was chaos in the hall. I went to the green room to give everyone their costumes and told them to put it on. The green room was filled with students who were getting ready. All looked amazing. I could make out some of the main characters from other plays like Julius Caesar and the dusky skinned Othello. Some characters went on to rehearse dialogues in front of the mirror while some changed to get ready. The room was getting suffocated and my nervousness increased. I bent over feeling very weak. The chaos started giving me panic attacks and I ran out of the green room into the audience and out through the gate to find some place to sit alone.

I looked around and found a bench 15 feet from the main staircase behind which there were only trees and bushes. Noises from the auditorium reached there too but I couldn't go very far away. So I sat on the half-broken green bench with my manuscript in my hand slouching, my hair blowing in the wind as the birds chirped above me. The dim lights around made me feel better. It was natural for me to run away when I was scared. I had always been doing that. I couldn't handle pressure. I had given up athletics due to the fear of running with six other people in lanes next to me. I was a fast runner, but an extremely scared one. The wait in the lane before the gunshot made me sick. Giving up on running was way better than facing that.

I closed my eyes and started distracting my mind with other things like chocolate mousse and waffles, and then big bang theory and Paris Hilton.

I started thinking about how it would be to meet a person like Sheldon Cooper from the *Big Bang Theory* in real life or how it would be to love a person who had cancer like Augustus loved Hazel in *The Fault in Our Stars*.

"You can open your eyes now", and there was Rehaan again, sitting next to me and staring. I just could never talk when he was around. I liked to be pricy and unknown to him. It made US interesting. He hardly spoke to me one-on-one, but boys in general were like that. Also the amount of talking I did in my head made it hard for me to actually talk to him when he was around. He would always find me. Always start coming around. Something that was certainly questionable. He held my hand and got up, looked back and smiled at me as I got up and took me through the stairs that were now being covered with thick glossy red colour. He made me sit down in the middle of an empty row and sat next to me. "We'll sit here till we have to get ready. Don't worry", he assured me. I did as he said. It made me feel better.

Ours was the third performance so we sat to watch the first play *Taming of the Shrew* by Orient School until Mrs. Mary came looking for us furiously and asked us to go get ready immediately. We ran like kids who were reprimanded.

The curtains opened for the play as I stood in the wings. I could see a number of people staring at the stage persistently. I could not see an empty chair. A huge pendulum wall clock stood on the crimson painted wall at the end of the hall.

I entered the stage and played my part as best as I could. My heart thumped faster than usual. It was the fright of performing among so many people under the spotlight. I kept all my fear aside for the sake of all the hard work put by the students and Mrs. Mary. I was playing the lead role and had great responsibility.

Everything went as expected other than the cardboard-painted tree that fell down accidently during Rahil's speech. That was a total drawback but we were trained to act like nothing happened. The nervousness slowly ran out and I began enjoying my performance. The long full-length yellow dress that I wore gave me confidence; it was designed by me after all. Rehaan's performance was at ease and we delivered our dialogues with a lot of love and affection. It almost seemed like we felt what we were saying. The impression I had of Rehaan's inability to express emotions was cynical when he performed the scene where he was told Juliet was dead. The heart-breaking climax of the story, I hoped, had moved our audience and judges.

After all the performances from all the schools, we patiently heard the judge as he spoke,

"We are thoroughly surprised by the high level of integrated performance of these young talents. Each play was well performed and executed to its highest level of credentials. Each performance was certainly incredible. For us all the teams are winners but as we all know we have to decide a winner. The play, by a thin line, as best play goes to Westwood International's *Romeo and Juliet*!

This dramatics as a whole had given me a lot: my bonding over friendships, my public speaking skill enhancement, my first designed pieces of cloth, my new best friend Rehaan and of course the large gold cup-shaped trophy that had my name engraved on it.

Chapter 4

Sugar-coated Success

"Alexander McQueen and Valentino Garavani at flat 50% off only for today", said the sign board outside Chilson Mall in France where I stood in line with plenty other women awaiting my turn to make use of the sale. As I got in, I picked up four different dresses that were somehow only appropriate for the Oscars. I moved on to pick up two Jimmy Choo pumps and Christian Dior make-up items when suddenly whispers fell on my eardrums.

"Wake up Aria", I blinked my half-open swollen eye repeatedly to tell myself I wasn't in France and still had to buy my Jimmy Choos.

It had been a few weeks since the shooting and I believe this was the first time since that horrible day that I was blessed with sound sleep. I wasn't even completely out of bed when I saw the corners of my room had Rahil and Rehaan play Xbox One, which I purchased because it looked good, and in the other corner was Jay complaining about how huge and expensive my walk-in wardrobe was. That was how close we all had come in the past few years. These maniacs were my life now. The finest people I could have asked for, always by my side and undoubtedly more entertaining than watching Tom and Jerry.

"I've got some good news", said Kiara

"What!!!! You're pregnant?" I laughed

"No you idiot, there's a letter for you, open it".

Perplexed I snatched the typed out letter from her hand ignoring my decision to first brush my teeth. I read it silently and the others started coming around. As I progressed through the lines my eyes became moist.

"Yes Aria, Forever 21 wants you to design clothes for them. Not only did they see your work at the intercollegiate dramatics last year but also went through all your sketches.

"What? How did my sketches even reach them?" I asked baffled at the invasion of my privacy.

"When the chairperson and head of marketing at Forever 21 came to our school they met Mrs. Mary asking them about you and your designs and Rehaan informed them that you even had sketches that you made during your leisure time".

Rehaan smiled at me while finding a perfect place for his butt on my maroon bean bag.

Kiara added "They were interested in your designs and wanted to have a meeting with you. We held this for so long to surprise you today and also so that you move on from the shooting day because the police department is on their toes and have been successful in finding a few clues about the criminals".

I was in the middle of a lot of mixed feelings. I was overwhelmed that I received an offer like this but was confused at the same time at the thought of why they would want me to design clothes for them. I didn't have a course in fashion designing or a completed degree or any experience in mainstream designing.

I looked at Rehaan innocently. The intercom in my room rang and my mom called all of us down for breakfast.

"Rehaan wait", I said as he was just about to leave after everyone else. I was in a dilemma.

"Should I do this?"

"Why would you question it?" he answered questioningly.

"I don't think dad will like it. He would tell me to go buy Forever 21 but not slog and work under someone. I'm scared".

He interrupted my speech in the middle to add "Aria it doesn't matter how much money you have or how many things you can buy, this is about you, and how your art and talent could make a difference. It's about what you can do on your own. You have a passion for fashion and you should follow it. It all starts from scratch. So you have to work hard". He came closer and looked deeply into my eyes, close enough for me to hear his heartbeat. His thick and plum lips were as red as a tomato, his skin as clear as milk.

"You've been brought up in the most sheltered life that I know of and you need to step out of it to prove yourself and see life. I know that you can do it because" and he took a long pause "I believe in you".

There was magic in his sentences and a glow in his eyes. I somehow fell in love with every word that he said and wanted him to repeat them over and over again. He was more than my best friend and always less than a boyfriend. My adviser, my guide, my support system. Someone I could say anything to. He was also the coolest person I had known. Spoke less, spoke well, unlike me who would say anything that came into my mind. He was very hard working. He was, as every teenager is, extremely confused about everything, but once he made a decision there was no going back. He was an outgoing person, loved travelling and adventure. He was also very reserved at times, he had his close group of friends that he always liked around him.

Monday morning was fixed for my meeting. I wore my Charlotte Russe lace net white top with jet black Armani leggings. Blue eyeliner made my eyes pop so I put a nude brown lipstick to tone down the look. How self-obsessed I was, I thought to myself. I organized my bag with all essentials for the day and was extremely confident about winning this deal and impressing the company.

They took me into their huge cabin where a nice lady introduced herself as Preeti and asked me a few questions about myself as she walked me around the office. The office was huge, almost like a mall. The divisions all throughout were made by glass, so every person's work and whereabouts were openly seen. People ran around from one corner to another with files in their hands and blazers on their torso.

She took me to the conference room where three middle-aged men were sitting around the round table in black suits and papers in their hands. They began to ask me "How have you been since the shooting day at school?" I figured they knew it through the papers and news channels.

"I told them I was better".

"Tell us in one word what fashion means to you?" Asked one of the gentlemen.

"Attitude".

What do you expect from this job? The questions kept coming in.

I was absolutely unprepared for an interview.

"I expect to learn about fashion and business", I answered, hesitantly.

"But you claim to know fashion".

"There's no limit to learning".

"At this age, how would you handle working with other known fashion designers and models?"

"With patience. I think it is very important to understand that firstly, they are all older than me and secondly they are all more experienced. So by keeping my point across sternly and by also being open to new ideas and criticism, I would be able to effectively deal with them".

"What does Forever 21 depict to you?"

This was my favourite question.

"Forever 21 has not only been a student-friendly affordable brand but it is also one of the trendiest brands that ranges from daily wear to high-end lifestyle clothing. I love the fact that Forever 21 understands exactly what the 21 year old requires in terms of clothes, accessories and footwear".

I spoke to them about my love for fashion for over half an hour. How I loved everything that had to do with fashion and designing. I told them about the blogs I wrote and the responses to it. They keenly observed all my sketches that I showed to them while they nodded their heads to my speech over fashion.

The next day I was called again.

On the basis of the designs of the costumes I made for Romeo and Juliet and my sketches they wanted me to design a *Spring Summer Collection* for them. Not only that but they would also line me up at their upcoming fashion show and make me the face of Forever 21 for that collection. They also mentioned that they were taking me as a brand face because of my father's name who was one of the city's biggest business tycoons. They wanted a face to represent the youth and their sense of fashion.

"A lot of young girls would want to dress up and wear clothes that girls brought up like you would".

I was glad they made this clear in the beginning. I didn't think much because I was delighted. I went home to announce this to my mother and she was very happy. She said she would talk to dad about it and I didn't need to worry at all. She sharply reminded me that the major reason they were taking me was because I was Oberio's daughter and I should never forget that.

I couldn't wait to start making sketches keeping in mind what the youth would wear for summer. Bold, trendy and out-of-the-box were on the top of my list.

My designs were sent to the client's office as and when I completed making them. They began promoting it soon enough. It was officially announced on their site that I would be launching a new line and they began updating it everywhere on social network with my pictures on it. A sneak peak was allowed to be given by me on my instagram with about two of the pieces once they were made. I then did a photo shoot where I wore the clothes I designed to be placed in magazines and hoardings across the city. They were investing a large sum of money on this, but it was obvious that only then would people buy those clothes. I gave a few interviews for magazines where I spoke about my line, seventeen being my ultimate favourite. They all asked me how it started and what I see in the coming days. I always had to think a lot before giving my answers and be politically correct about it.

In this amazing limelight the launch day arrived in no time. I was supposed to be at the Forever 21 store in the Infinity Mall for the launch and I thought maybe five or ten people would turn up to see the line.

The turnout though blew my mind off. I couldn't count how many girls were outside the store when I was inside. I had bouncers surrounding me. I didn't know marketing and promotion could make so much of a difference. I was nervous at the launch, everyone wanted to take pictures with me. But I wasn't even a celebrity. I was delighted and overwhelmed, all at the same time. I gave a lengthy speech in front of all the people, mostly comprising girls, that was prepared by Forever 21.

Forever 21 added my line to the stock and made me a permanent designer looking at the success of the launch. My instagram followers increased every time I signed in. My *facebook* was flooded with messages. Everything was happening so fast. I was overwhelmed. I couldn't believe it was so easy to be famous. I was a public figure now and not known only because of my father but now on my own. All of it at this age was unexpected for me. I was called by *Fashion Time* magazine for their June cover page with an exclusive interview on how it all began. I would never forget to mention that Rehaan was the extra push I needed for the belief in myself to be able to do something.

Looking at the response my father was extremely supportive of me unlike what I thought his reaction would be. He said that he didn't have any problem and he's always been strict with me so that I would know how to differentiate right from wrong. He was a man of principles, always doing what was meant to be. He taught me many things, most of all to be honest. I didn't see him much during my growing up days. He was a really busy man and of course, you don't become a millionaire without working every hour that you can. I loved the fact that he always appreciated me, mom didn't as much, but he snapped at me often. The workload being the culprit!

I was given a personal assistant by Forever 21 to help me in all my work. After the contract-signing amount, cheques of a percent of the sales were sent to me. I started making appearances at events and fashion shows with an overwhelming media inquisitive about everything I did.

I now had a financial consultant and a PR team, that my mom closely worked with, an assistant and a bodyguard that my dad insisted, all working under me. I didn't socialize much now; most of my time went in working and the rest with my group.

I got my next offer immediately. Forever 21 was displaying their lines at the IMS Fashion Show 2012 and my new collection was proposed to be displayed on the ramp before it went on the racks.

Amidst preparing clothes for my show, something strange happened one evening. The bell rang and my servant said someone asked for me. At my doorstep stood Priyana Jha.

If I had to describe her in one line, she was the most arrogant and superficial person whom no one liked in all of college. She always made nasty comments on every girl and put them down. She was a bully and many faced problems because of her. I had a bitter fight with her back in middle school when she called me a bimbo. I had never spoken to her since then. I hated even looking at her and here she stood in front of me, face bent down looking at my huge silver doormat. She was way taller than me but she slouched and stood with all her weight on one leg. She looked up to me when I asked her with my eyebrows raised "yes?" She wore thick black full framed spectacles that covered almost all of her tiny little face, her hands hidden behind her Burberry shawl that covered her torso. Her body was as lifeless as could be. It looked as though her skin rested on her bones with no flesh in between. Her eyes, with the deepest dark circles kept watering, as I was still wondering what was happening here.

"What happened?" I asked her.

"Can I come in?" She said

I took her to my room and made her sit down. She looked like she was in a lot of trouble.

With a sorry face and a heavy manly voice she spoke, "I have nowhere to go, my parents have disowned me, I don't have a life and I don't know what to do".

"Wait wait wait. How about we start from the beginning? Why all this?" I asked.

"I've been using drugs and I cannot leave them, I'm helpless without it. My parents found out and after a huge brawl, have thrown me out. I've been falling sick and have been having hallucinations. I can't concentrate on anything and all my friends have left me. I have no hope left".

I raised my eyebrows and asked "Why would you come to me, when you hate me and you know I hate you?"

She sobbed even more now "I know I'm a bad person and I know you're not, that's why".

She took a sip of water and wiping her nose she continued "I just wanted a little money because I know you have been working on your own and only you can give me some. I want to rent a house".

I went ahead to console her as she completely broke down, my mind simultaneously thinking about why I would help someone I hated. I didn't want her to suffer like this. I wouldn't wish that for anyone, or regret that I didn't help her. She was the kind to hate and pity at the same time but I thought I would help her to make her a different person. I gave her some money and told her I would see what I could do to help.

Once she left I called my agent and asked if I could recommend a model. He said he would have to check with Forever 21 and she would do the needful. I gave him Priyana's number to forward all her details and pictures.

Sometimes you have to go outside your box. Outside of what's comfortable. See where good deeds leave you, how to handle what's important and set your priorities straight.

Glamorous glittering nights were part of my life but this one was particularly special and extremely close to my heart. Everything I dreamt of was right in front of me. Famous designers, luxury clothes, fashionable VIPs and a grand fashion show. The center of the hall had a huge silver glittering ball that hung four feet from the ceiling. It had small pieces of glass all around it reflecting the light to all different corners. The round stage ramp ended right in the middle of the hall. The theme of the decoration was white. There were about thirty round tables covered with white cloth having white flowers in vases at the center. Eight chairs surrounded each table. The ramp cloth was in diagonal shades of white and red. The music here, for a change, was soothing, slow and relaxing.

I started preparing my models with their final fittings and checking if all their clothes were appropriately placed on them. Models, I realized, were very true to what they are projected. They appeared to not understand the hassle they were creating. Some kept smoking, some spoke on their phones, others were too high, and all of this while changing into their costumes. Very unprofessional I thought. There was only one thing I was really anxious about. My clothes were simple elegant every day wear. Extremely different from the ones that models wore on the ramp. I didn't know how people would perceive that.

Priyana at one end of the corner of the green room looked at me and smiled. She lifted up her fingers and joined the thumb to her index finger to tell me that she loved the outfit she was wearing. She moved her lips without speaking "thank you". I nodded my head. Everything was perfect.

My name was called out and the music for my models' walks slowly set in motion. They started walking the ramp with no emotions on their face. I always wondered why models had to keep a straight face and walk the ramp. I would hope to see a fashion show one day where all the models would be laughing and smiling through their way on the ramp. It went faster than I had expected. They came in, threw my first set of clothes while changing into the next and went back on. They really shouldn't disrespect my clothes, I was emotionally attached to these precious pieces. Priyana walked the ramp for the first time. I wanted her to be the show stopper but the company refused. The wanted someone experienced and well known as the show stopper. My show stopper design was a little different from the rest. I made it a little more complex. I basically kept in mind parties to which teenagers would go to and dress up their age, which was rare in our society. I wanted teenagers to dress like themselves and not like twenty-five year olds, so I designed a peacock blue colour knee-length net dress that fringed from the stomach and flew towards the knees. To give it a special touch I added gold jewels on the neck to make it look accessorized and covered the end of the sleeve in a thin line with the same jewels. I secretly made Kiara wear it before the show and she looked stunning in it. At the end of the display I was taken to the stage and my confidence was zero. I was scared and it showed on my face behind my smile. I saw everyone cheering and clapping all throughout. I was beyond nervous.

As I went back to the room Priyana held my hand, "I owe you Aria, thanks a lot, for this and the money", she said.

"It's okay, God probably gave you a second chance through me, just please don't go back and make the most of your life now", I answered.

I walked out astounded to see cameras flashing their lights endlessly at me and trying to fix their mikes right to my mouth with countless ambiguous questions that made it hard for me to understand even one of them correctly. In the core of this anxiousness I was mostly irritated about my phone constantly vibrating. I excused myself to a corner away from the noise and saw sixteen missed calls from my mother. I called her back and she spoke in a broken voice. "Sit in the car and come to the hospital immediately". "What happened?" I asked. She hung up. Next thing I know was security taking me out of the hall to my car. I was scared to death. Why would she call me to the hospital? The driver took me to Breach Candy and I saw people standing outside the hospital with cameras. The bodyguard then took me to the third floor. The sense of fright made my hands shiver. Everyone around looked worried.

Chapter 5

Hidden Unhidden Truths

My mom sat on the bench outside the ICU and cried and cried. I went towards the ICU door mystified and stood outside the glass door, impassive. Between all the doctors I saw a peek of my father lying down motionless on the bed being treated by the doctors. My mom walked to me and held me to almost cover me, but I couldn't feel what I was feeling. The walls around me started moving, my head spun and I fell down.

"I'm sorry baby, your father had a terrible accident at Worli sea face an hour back; they couldn't save him", crying my mother said as my eyes opened. I could see how hard the words were for her to say. She was lifeless; her skin was turning pale and blue. Her eyes looked so tired she could hardly open them.

Shattered was a small word. I felt undefined pain in my heart that I couldn't explain. I lay in bed crying with my mother next to me. I hardly could understand anything. I could just feel the pain. The pain that felt like my heart was coming out of my body, the pain that felt like needles poked me. The pain that consistently took me away from me.

My world broke into pieces within minutes. I was angry. Very angry. This wasn't justifiable. I always assumed mostly old people die. My father was young. He didn't deserve to die. It wasn't his time to die. He had more to live and more to do. How could God just take away someone's life so randomly? There was so much he still wanted to do. There was so much I wanted to do for him and with him and now he just won't ever be there? I could never see him again? I could never talk to him? This wasn't fair. My soul had thirst, my body anger! My fingers were senseless while my mind wandered. It's not easy to let someone go. It's not easy to say goodbye. But God didn't even seem to give me a chance.

Death doesn't ask you, neither does it tell you. It only takes away. Takes away painfully. Leaves you with life's greatest pain, life's greatest regrets. You don't have the ability to stop it, or to turn it around, but what you can do is learn. Learn to let go, learn to be strong, learn that nothing is permanent in this temporary world. Learn to do everything you want and wait for nothing because life doesn't wait, life is unpredictable. So when you think life is too long and you could wait for a few days, and then a few months, or a few years, you tell yourselves that life is what it is right now, life is what you make of right now.

I was constantly surrounded by people who cried all the time and even if I chose not to cry I would cry looking at them. My house was flocked by people before even I could enter. There were relatives, relatives of relatives, media, friends, family friends, my friends, their families and also the people who lived around. I wanted to be at peace alone, so I could feel remorse and regret how terrible I felt. But in this environment, that wasn't an option. The most pain I felt was because there was so much I wanted to tell my father before I couldn't. So much to thank him for, so much to ask and so much to let go. Mainly I just wanted him to know how much I loved and appreciated him. That day I should have stayed with dad. Not let him drive the car or how I hoped he wasn't going back home from office alone. I wish I could change something, anything. My father's body lay still with a picture above it. I sank my face in front of him and cried my heart out. The body was losing colour and turning pale. I couldn't watch the sight.

My friends took me to the room, consoled me but let me cry. Food didn't seem to go down my throat that day and it was almost like I didn't blink an eyelid that night. Next morning the body was taken away. What was left was now his things for us to see and remember but none of that would make a difference.

Days passed with me staring at the antique pendulum clock on the wall of my room or sitting in the balcony watching the birds fly. I sometimes stood in front of my father's things for hours sulking in his memories. I would then wear his watch and stand, wear his over-large size tuxedo and hold his pen pretending to write just like he did. My mother fell extremely ill. The doctors came and put her on glucose every now and then. They regularly checked her BP and gave her medicines. I had to be strong to look after her. I know she regretted it more. She regretted fighting with him when she could have spent time improving her relationship with him just before he left. They were a great couple but problems crushed them. Their regular fights had turned nasty and they decided to live separately for a few months. Dad stayed away and that's what she regretted the most. She realized how much she loved him.

A few days later a prayer meeting was held for my father's soul to rest in peace. Everyone was invited. I had no interest in attending it. I didn't want to see anyone's face.

Aunt Sara came to clean my room and saw me lying in bed, "Why aren't you coming down?" She asked.

"Why should I? What should I do there? Meet and see people cry like they were my father's best friends? Some of them down didn't even know my father properly; some are the ones who would talk behind his back and others would hardly be interested in knowing how his life was".

A shocked Aunt Sara replied almost irritably, "If you don't meet someone regularly doesn't mean that they careless about you or love you differently. Life is such, life is long and life is busy. Not everyone is able to meet everyone every day. People drift apart. Work, family, education. Distance is always created, and this distance is what tells you how you can be far apart and change nothing. There still are going to be people who knew your father; however, what they felt about him doesn't concern you because this isn't about you. It's about him". She left the room rather pissed off.

I decided to get ready and go down. I walked down the stairs with my hands sliding down the railing. That's what my father always did. He either had a cup of coffee in his hand or his cell phone but the other hand always slid down the railing when he walked down like a king – my king!

As I walked down my eyes got stuck to only one girl in the entire living area. She was crying incessantly over my dad's picture, her voice increasing every breath she took. I walked closer to see her but she wouldn't face up. Her back faced me. She looked around my age. Her wavy hair just touched her shoulders. She wore a white kurti that I could tell was from Zara, with white leggings that finished just before her ankle. Her brown jute bag was kept next to her. Her toes pointing out towards us were ugly. She had huge feet, incomparable to her short height and broad shoulders. She bent a little, her back still facing us and she looked at the picture of my father and covered her face with her hands. I wondered why she cried as though she had lost a father.

Her turning around, however, was a scandalous affair. Not something I could digest. She had the same face, the same eyes, the same nose and an even similar face as me.

What????? Was I watching a movie? Or was I dreaming in my dreams. The entire crowd was bowled over by her looks. I went closer to her to see clearly. Blinked my eyes a few times. She didn't say a word. She had pimples on her face unlike me. Her hair was half the length of mine and her skin tone was one shade lighter than mine. Everything else perhaps, was the same. How could two different people look alike? I have seen this happening only in movies. It was hard to digest someone looked like me. I wasn't over my dad's death and here, there was another shock on my platter, served with a cherry on top.

I took a glimpse at my mom and returned to ask her directly "Who are you, why are you crying so much?"

"I lost my father", she answered.

Now what pure rubbish was this? I thought to myself. Spellbound I looked at her and tried to fill her words in my mind. I looked around searching for my mom to explain this to me but I saw her walking towards the washroom crying remorsefully. As I walked closer to this girl she picked up her jute bag and walked towards the door. Everyone else stood still in their places and saw her leave. I thought she was completely insane and was in a state of shock or on high dose of some chemical drug to call my father hers.

The prayer meeting was long, really really long. Those chanting prayers remained in my head way after they were over. The huge hall was filled with people. Everyone sat on the floor in rows of five, one behind the other, all with sad faces and white clothes. After the prayer all of them came towards the family members to show their condolences. I was naturally only thinking about the girl with the same face as mine. I didn't even wait for everyone to leave and reached my mom asking her furiously about who this girl was and if she knew anything about her.

My mother took me to her bedroom quietly and made me sit. I figured that my mother knew something that she hadn't told me. The room reminded me more of my father. They lived in this room happily all the while that I was growing up. The bright red walls had now become dull for me, his laughing pictures all around the room were now only pictures. The silk white bed sheet I remember was his favourite.

My mom began, "Aria when you were born, you were not born alone". My head glided down and my eyeballs rolled up as I looked at my mother with intensity while she continued. "Do you remember Aunt Warda?" Amaira, who came home yesterday, is your twin sister. Your aunt took her away from me when you were born". She paused at my fuming reaction and then continued "My second ultrasound scan during the 19th week confirmed that I was going to be a mother of two. We were overjoyed with happiness and the pregnancy went smoothly until that stormy thundering night that I went into unbelievably strong labour pain for more time than expected. The pain was torturous, I screamed like my house was on fire. I thought I couldn't do it much longer. Your father stayed, helped and made it better. Your father was a totally different person back then. The pain was so unbearable that I hardly remember what was happening. The doctor said I may have complications and I had started bleeding a lot; so they recommended to your father that I have a cesarean delivery. The pain killers and then the anesthesia made me lose consciousness and after twenty minutes of continuous pain you finally came into this world, beautiful and fine-looking. A minute later your sister Amaira was born too. You were identical twins. I held both of you in my hand and it was the most special feeling I had ever experienced in my entire life. Your dad came and sat next to me looking at both of you like he looked at the most beautiful thing he had ever seen. I saw his eyes twinkle and his face with the broadest smile ever.

The doctor mumbled something to the nurse and took both the kids away. They were probably taking you both for cleaning and medications. A ton of people swept into the room after a while to congratulate us but I was still in a lot of pain to thank everyone and smile at them. The doctor called your father out for a while when I spoke to my family. Once the visiting hours were over your father came in with a long face. I asked him what happened. He pressed his lips under his teeth and said to me that only one of our children had survived, the second child had died soon after the delivery but they couldn't tell me at that time. I was devastated".

"How is she alive suddenly then?" I yelled.

My mom tried to consolingly reply to me "We came to know two years back that your aunt bribed the doctor to give her one child when she came to know I was having twins. She took her far away, settled with her husband and never came back. Her incapability to have children led her to such desperate act".

"Are you justifying her act? Are you telling me she stole a human being and you did nothing and the hospital did nothing and the doctor got away? You knew since two years that my twin sister is alive and you do not bother to tell me a thing until she turns up crying when my father dies?"

"I'm not justifying her act" she said "your father and I were waiting for the correct time to tell you this; we didn't know how you would process or understand these things at such an immature age".

"I'm an adult, if you guys can fight in front of me all the time then I think I've gone through enough". I raged out of the room, stamping my foot violently.

I was already going through an emotional turmoil with my father's death, regretting things I should have told him and now I learn that my mother hides things from me that I should know, hides the fact that I have a twin sister and an aunt who's a bitch. I don't know how many more secrets she had kept from me.

Next day Amaira was there again; this time with a white shirt, light pink painted nails and a huge mustard color file in her hand. Her hair tied in a pony. Next to her walked a tall middle-aged man with broad shoulders, wheatish skin and large round glasses that rested on his big swollen like nose. He wore a black suit and carried a laptop bag in his hand. I fled to my mom, still as angry as yesterday, and asked her now what new scene this was. "I don't know", she said and walked towards them.

Amaira then suddenly spoke in a shrill voice "In the events of the happenings of this family, I would like to take note of what carries most importance. I have not come here to interfere in your lives as I have no significance but it is a must that we have ourselves free from each other in matters of law. I have come here to fairly settle the property of my father, and my part in it".

"Excuse me? Stop calling my father yours and you do not have any share in any property. You can't turn up one fine day and ask for rights that are not yours". It was almost like I was blasting her. I was a very blunt person. I said whatever came to my mind. I was very harsh in my opinions too, but I said the truth, always!

"Laws are funny Aria" her shrill voice itched in my ears "they don't go according to sentiments and emotions, I'm the biological daughter of Mr. Oberio and I'm as much part of the property as you are. We are here to discuss the property, its value and division, please cooperate. The rest would be explained by my lawyer Mr. Rajesh Tripathi".

I took my mom aside and asked her "Now what?"

"Stop panicking", she said.

She spoke to them rather calmly, "I will talk to my lawyer and get back to you tomorrow".

That evening our lawyer Mr. Mirchandani was called home. He was an old man and by the amount of grey hair on his head it was evident how experienced he was. His face was full of wrinkles and his lose skin fell off from his chin. He had a rather annoying habit of talking at an accelerated speed and tone. I would generally never understand what he said, as he always spoke in numbers, but his fast pace of speech made it harder for me to comprehend even his basics. He was our lawyer, family friend and also our financial advisor. He wore a worried face that day. Came home and sat down on the large red sofa and kept his office bag down. "We need to talk", he said to us. Mom and I looked at each other.

He hesitantly spoke to us "Mr. Oberio was indeed a great man and a greater entrepreneur. We all know about his great business skills through his wealth and various acquisitions throughout these years. Recently though, due to some faulty decisions taken by Mr. Oberio, his fate has rested in the hands of God".

I wish he'd just come to the point, I thought to myself.

"I will try to be as simple in my business terms as possible for you to break down the complexity of the business he dealt in. As we know there are three major mines in his name in the state of Madhya Pradesh. The mines we went to see in Jhalawar mainly produce *kota* stones. Apart from all his major business ventures which included stocks, construction, gold etc., this was a superior one. The money he made in these mines was tremendous and for the past five years these mines have been extremely beneficial for him. The problem arose a year ago, when a diamond mine proposition came his way. There's a diamond mine in Panna in Madhya Pradesh that was proposed to Mr. Oberio to buy. He asked me whether he should or not as the investment was huge. The investment included almost all the profits from the other businesses. I told him the basic layout, the work required and the amount to be invested. I told him that it required a huge sum of money to be invested so it was a huge risk to take. I could tell the business aspects to the proposal but the choice was in his hands and he decided to go for it".

He paused to take a sip of coffee that Raju kept near him and then continued "buying that mine needed a lot of money; he invested a lot from his personal savings and also from the profits of all his other businesses. He still required more money and he took a loan from the bank and the loan was huge. He mortgaged his extra properties and a lot of gold against the loan. He was sure to make double the amount in time and he was extremely eager about this mine. In about two to three months all the paper work was ready and Mr. Oberio went to visit the mine. The digging had started. The mine was huge and spread over 9.5 kilometers. But then something terrible happened. After two months of continuous digging almost to the bottom all that was found was stones and no diamonds; the deeper they dug to the bottom the more frustrated Mr. Oberio became. The mine turned out to be empty and there were no diamonds in it. When this was announced to Mr.

Oberio, he went into a state of shock and depression. He went into hiding and was not seen for 14 days after that. It was natural. He was the sole reason for the huge unpredictable loss. He stayed at a hotel without telling anyone, but he couldn't hide forever. He was a strong man and had to take the responsibilities of his actions. He decided that he needed to face his problems. He first paid a lot of money to not make this a public affair. He then, sat with me, put all his money together and how much he would have to pay back. This was going to be his life's largest loss. We just had to estimate how much greater the loss would be than expected. In short, the loan took away his properties and his gold. He had to sell of most of his things and within six months most of his earnings had gone down drastically. His lifestyle, including his expenditure for you both caused more problems because saving was hard to do. He did not reveal all this to anybody and kept it hidden. His properties that made money were given to the bank for not paying back the loan; therefore his income sources were now belittled. He didn't want to tell you both and told me strictly to not say anything as he didn't want you both to suffer as he was still finding a way out of this so that things would become better".

I turned around to mom, she looked around hazily, stood up, bent over and suddenly fell to the ground. The entire house workers and the few guests that were around picked her up and splashed water on her. I called for the doctor immediately. This was too much tragedy for one family at one time. I didn't want to face this. I couldn't afford anything happening to my mother now. She woke up partially and we put her to sleep.

Chapter 6

Glitches in Society

All of dad's properties were sold and a lot of it was seized. Within a month the company's offices and cars were sold. It became a public affair as we now read them through the papers and saw them on news channels. There was no one left to handle of what little was left. My mom had her reserves in jewellery and gold but I didn't know how long that would last. My calculations were really bad anyways. I was Ishan Awasti, the dyslexic boy from *Taare Zameen Par*, when it came to numbers. Everyone referred to him to explain my intolerance towards numbers. Our lawyer Mr. Mirchandani suggested that we put this house on rent and shift to another area where the prices were lower as it was necessary to have a major fixed income. I outrightly denied his proposition out of self-interest.

"Mom! This is dad's house, we can't leave it. Where will we go so suddenly and how will we adjust. This is dad's house and he bought it with a lot of pain and tremendous attachment to it. It's almost like he build this house brick by brick. It was his heart and soul and this is the worst thing you can do after he's gone".

"I know, but we don't have an option. Calm down!" She said. "We have to be practical, we aren't selling it. We are putting it on rent and we can have it back when things are better".

My mother, with the help of a few brokers, looked around for houses in Mumbai and managed to find a two thousand square feet flat in Grant Road. I had only crossed that area to go elsewhere. It was too tacky for me. I just hoped they didn't finalize it. I was taken to see the flat without my consent.

The area was much of a mess if I put it across politely. Firstly, it was obnoxiously noisy, which was a major problem as I was used to silence, silence for everything I did and for everything I wanted to do. Secondly, the building was old and creepy. Scraps of the wall hung out from everywhere with eagles and probably even vultures having their nests secured for years as I could tell by the state of the building. The white colour of the building hid behind the dirt all over it. The building had just one watchman at a time to look after it. The watchman was an interesting soul himself. He lifted his right hand to his forehead, his fingers together pointing at his head with the palm facing outward towards us as he saluted. "Salaam" he said and spread his one acre long smile to show off his teeth that were red with the *paan* he stored in one side of his palate. I entered the lift to a strong foul smell and immediately covered my nose with my hand. Fourth floor had three flats. 401 was for sale. The three bedroom-hall-kitchen that I entered to glance at seemed to finish before it even began. Two big rooms and a tiny one! Nothing compared to my old house. I wondered who would be renting our bungalow and how they would maintain it. There were only two bathrooms. The flat was well kept and better than I imagined it to be after comparing it to the condition of the building. I wanted us to shift elsewhere but my mom said this was perfect as the price of this building would increase once a builder would buy it and make a new building here. I had lost the ability to be objective by now. I asked my mom how all my stuff would fit in this tiny house and to my sudden surprise she said we wouldn't be taking everything.

Leaving my bungalow was heart breaking, moreover at the time when I needed stability in my life. It's a funny thing, what situations life can throw at you and make you adjust to. Shifting to an area that was so different from ours was scary. It was hard for my mother more than it was for me and she put up with it really strongly. We shifted within a week and our belongings kept coming in cartons slowly. The house was fully furnished before we came but we changed a few things according to our needs. I got a new pink wardrobe and arranged all my stuff in my room. I took the tiny extra room also for all my clothes and bags and shoes and still found the place to be inadequate for all my possessions. There was still a lot of stuff unpacked. Rehaan came over a few days later. He had a unique gait, legs walked far away from each other and toes pointed outwards, something that always reminded me of Fred Flintstones. I asked him where the others were. He said nothing. We sat and spoke about my shifting for a bit after which his talks turned serious.

"Aria, I know you have been going through a lot and life has been hard on you recently but you need to get back to your daily life and daily chores. You haven't attended college in three months, the teachers have been asking about you. We'll have our exams coming up soon. You need to cover up a lot. I'm there to help you though". I keenly observed the movements of his hands while he spoke, his hand gestures were almost as though mute people explained what they were trying to say. It was his habit. Then my thoughts lingered on what he said. He was right. I had to go to college.

Monday. The day of the week everyone always cribbed about. The first time after three months I decided to go to college. I asked my mom for my pocket money. She swirled through her heart-shaped purse kept on the round center table in the hall right under the ceiling fan and removed a few thousand notes. It didn't take time for me to count them. I placed them back in her palm.

"What are you doing mom?" I said, in a higher than normal decibel.

"That's for a month".

"Only ten thousand rupees?" "You know that's how much I would spend in two days. I need more", I was yelling by the end of my sentence.

"Aria, we have to stay on a budget now, we don't have so much money, and you have to cut down on your expenditure", she asserted.

I put the money on the table and left home banging the door behind me. Only Rehaan came to my mind at that frustrated moment, so while I stood under my building, I called him to pick me up. The waiting period added on to my frustration. A glance at the entire street and I was completely horrified. From one end to another everyone looked at me and I wondered why, probably because I dressed in a classier way than them. I avoided it until two guys looked at me constantly and giggled. Then they said something to each other. I started walking towards them to do something about it; I don't know what but something. Maybe I would tell them to mind their own business or maybe yell at them. But before I could reach them, Rehaan stopped his Beemer right in front of me. I almost toppled on the bonnet losing my balance.

"What are you doing? Why did you get out? Don't walk here. Sit in the car" he said "you know you're not supposed to walk in these areas".

"I don't understand why, why would they look at me like that?" I walked towards the front passenger seat.

"Just listen to me and don't" he said.

I hoped college would change my mind, but this was an unforeseen dreadful day. We were both late for class so we sat down quietly listening to the lecture. I had not attended college for the past three months which was why I didn't understand a word that Manish Sir said. His beard annoyed me for some strange reason. He always wore a tie, something no other teacher ever did. He pointed his scale towards the class after every sentence he taught. "Do you understand?" his patented dialogue which most students mocked at after class. I turned around and saw Kiara, Rahil and Jay sitting behind together, I smiled at them. At recess I went behind and asked them if they wanted go to the cafeteria. They smiled at me. While I went to take my bag they started leaving without me. I don't know why they didn't wait for me. So I went down with Rehaan and looked for them. We all sat on our normal routine round table in the corner of the cafeteria away from the college building. Our cafeteria was less filled with physical items and full of intangible memories. It was a hub of all those laughters and jokes we cracked through the years. The USP of the cafeteria was its noise. I could never imagine this place silent. The dustbin there was an interesting piece of memory too. A lot of important items were thrown in it all throughout college. From my phone covers to important notes, anything my friends found important was laughingly thrown into the bin. They were such bullies, but what was friendship without some harmless bullying and ragging?

Kiara excused herself to get her food but went to sit with Sanjana and started eating. I just kept wondering what happened. I thought I would go there too. I took my food while Rehaan spoke to Rahil and Jay and went over to Kiara.

"How are you holding up?" She asked me

"Better. But I have loads to talk to you".

She smiled at me. We ate while she spoke to Sanjana. Something was weird, she hardly spoke to me that day but I didn't pay much attention. Rahil and Jay left without telling me. I was a little displeased at their behaviour that day and did not know how to ask them what was wrong. I constantly assumed that the problem was not with them but with me as I was still incompetent to face daily life and the matters that came with it. I was still not in the right frame of mind.

I sat to think of old days of when I was a kid and life was so uncomplicated. Life basically comprised playing in the lawn in front of my bungalow, eating and sleeping. Studies were much easier. Life was much simpler. I remembered a time from my childhood where I sat in the lawn making Lego blocks. I was about five or six. Mom and dad were on vacation. Aunt Sara was asleep in the kitchen that afternoon. I saw an airplane, the size of an insect, soaring high in the cloudless sky. I remember marking the difference of it looking at it from inside and from thousands of feet under it. Soon enough, I saw another plane on the other end of the sky, parallel to the first one, larger in size. I held my breath back before panicking. I pushed the ground with my hands and got up, ready to run and save the country from its biggest mishaps. I scuttled with naked feet on the freshly grown grass towards the entrance of my bungalow, which back then I called my Barbie house, and picked up the telephone dairy and receiver kept on the table simultaneously. "I have an emergency to report, sir" I said to some airport authority "there are two planes flying in the sky together, they are very close to each other and they will crash. Do something immediately".

Innocence is subtle, unrestrained, genuine and kind. It's selfless. It lacks guilt and bad intention. We are born with it, but we lose it through our journey in life. All the bad influences, bad situations and bad people get us scared. Scared of being ourselves and scared to live, in which we most efficiently lose the innocence we are born with.

I think of it now and laugh to myself, laugh at how I thought two planes couldn't fly in the sky together or they would crash. Laugh at how I called up some important authority and they had a good laugh at the naïveté of a five year old. Something about innocence I would never share with anyone is how I thought all dogs were males and all cats were females. Yes I did think so!

Rehaan came over later that day. Mom served him some chilly cheese toast and fish fingers with his favourite tartar sauce. He licked off his fair round structured fingers and dirtily wiped them off on his shorts. I was sketching a few clothes and deciding their colours when he softly spoke to me.

"I know you felt weird in college today".

"Umm yeah, how do you know?" I asked still looking down at my work. "Actually I wanted to say something to you".

"Yeah?"

"You know how our college is, and how our society is right?" he paused "Since everyone now knows about everything that happened with your father, they are likely to behave differently".

"Excuse me what? I sat up straight.

"Come again, what?" I said. "What are you trying to say, be specific?" I left all the sketches and sat at the edge of my wooden chair.

"Actually everyone at school is behaving differently with you because of whatever has happened with you. They don't see you the same way. You have shifted here and your lifestyle has changed. They all believe you don't belong with them anymore".

My eyes welled up with tears as I questioned "So if I shift to this area and don't have as much money as I had, my friends will leave me? Won't talk to me? Won't sit with me? Is that what you're saying?"

"See Aria, I don't believe in all this, that's why I'm still here, but you tell me how many friends do you have from the second or third category?"

"None right?"

I looked into his eyes. "I'M NOT FROM THE SECOND CATEGORY!"

"Look at you; you're getting offended even if I call you one".

"That's because they are different people, they come from different backgrounds and I'm still the same person", I said.

"See, this is the problem, you are still differentiating, and it's a fact that everyone does. They see you now as different from before".

But I still am the same person; those people were born that way and so they live differently than us". I knew in my mind I had no other justification.

"Calm down. Just give it some time". He said.

"Are you serious? Even Kiara and Jay and Rahil? That's totally impossible. Is it?"

By now I was so weak that if anyone did anything, it hurt me like needles poking my heart. I kept aside all my drawings and went to the bathroom to sob. My friends were ignoring me not because of something I did, but because of my circumstances. I would let myself believe that all of this was some major mistake, maybe they were being misinterpreted. But reality kept striking back. I was really being ignored.

The dramatic spirit that I was, I decided to go to Kiara and talk to her. I stood in front of her the next day and asked her for a full-fledged explanation to her behaviour at that very moment under the shade of the banyan tree outside the college. Her reply though, made the needles poke deeper. She said that after what happened to my company and my father, which was now on every tabloid, she said she had a reputation to maintain and she couldn't hang out with me anymore. What was more painful was her making me realize that I could now anyways not be a part of any plans because I had a fixed amount of money to spend and a lot more to save. She told me how I wouldn't be able to "afford" her so-called lifestyle.

Pain? Anger? Remorse? Nooooo. It was something I couldn't explain. I left without listening to anything more. I tried to hide my tears till I walked away with the feeling of being lonely more than being alone. I thought to myself if I'd push this any further then I would not be treated the way I wanted. Maybe I would be with them but not with respect. And I never allowed anyone to come between my dignity and self-respect.

Never in my wildest dream would I have thought that this was going to come from my closest friend of so many years. I was more baffled than angry. I didn't have the courage to deal with anything more she had to say to me, if at all she did. This was who I called my best friend who would stay forever. After her words I didn't have the nerve to listen to Jay and Rahil. Their words, I assumed, would be more blunt, and boys were not someone I could throw my emotions at or plead for friendship. Not something Aria Oberio ever did or ever will. I had too much class to confront them. I just wanted to be and stay alone. Again. Forever. My ego told me how I never would need them. I felt broken from inside. I hated change and I had no idea how I would adjust to this one now.

I would not deny the fact that I started feeling bad for all those children who ever faced this problem. I wondered how they would feel about being constantly judged on where they came from and being treated accordingly. Everyone wanted to be trendy and cool but that only came if you had a lot of money or you looked very good. The not so good were left alone, had no one and had no say. *I guess I realized that we feel the pain of others when we are put in the same situation.*

I decided I still had Rehaan and I didn't need anyone else. He was my world now and the fact that he was staying with me when no one was gave me heaps of courage. I would live my life normally like I would if this didn't happen. I always depended on him for everything. He was always there.

I went to college with a heavy heart the next day. The morning reminded me of how I ate breakfast with dad when he was there. He would drop me at college some days and teach me a few good lessons of life on the way. College was harder day by day – unexplainable behaviour of my batch mates. I generally sat alone and went back home immediately after, missing the long hours I spent in the college cafeteria. I went and sat there alone. Next to me was a table filled with snooty girls. I would talk to them sometimes. I stayed away because I knew they were very mean. They giggled and laughed constantly as I ate alone. One of them looked at me and pointed towards me telling her friends, if I heard correctly, "look at the poor Aria all alone these days, what she thought she'd be and what has she become. How sad!" she said sarcastically. They mocked and laughed. I got up and walked away, heard another girl remark at me "till when will you walk away?" by now their laugher echoed in the entire cafeteria. I was embarrassed in front of everyone. I couldn't retaliate with the thought of being their subject of fun anymore. I ran outside feeling restless and victimized. I reached home and wept in my mother's lap – wept until the sun set in the west. My phone rang and my mother answered. "It's Forever 21" she said. The manager called to ask me if my designs were complete. I told her I would take time. They wanted me to send my completed designs to them, immediately.

College days became harder and harder. Looking at Kiara was stressful. We couldn't look into each other's eyes, but every time I saw her I had a flashback of all those beautiful and fun moments we had. Things hurt more when I would see Rahil, Kiara, Rehaan and Jay together, walking past me like there was nothing between us ever. The worst kind of broken relations were the ones that happened over unsaid and unspoken situations. They felt so filled and empty at the same time. I had a million things to say to Jay and Rahil and maybe even to Kiara, but I just couldn't show my emotions and express my feelings in words. And that frustrated me the most. How could something so important just end like that? How could you just break a relation? Maybe for them, relations were something you could break over night – something that had very little meaning to them. But for me, I didn't know how to go away from someone or end things so abruptly. I didn't know how to switch from people and find new ones next day. I wish I wasn't so soft hearted. It wouldn't have hurt as much then.

Rehaan would come to me later and always tell me that he didn't want to stay away from me and he felt bad he couldn't change someone's mind. I always told him that he doesn't have to feel bad about being with them. He had the right to enjoy with them and I would never stop him to do so. Rehaan stayed with me every day. We became even closer. I would weep on his shoulder every day and he would handle all of my break downs. He would do everything he could to make me feel better. I appreciated it a lot. When he was around I never felt like I needed anything more. I was complete around him. I would always think of how hard it would be for him to stay with someone who was going through so much and still keep up with it.

One morning when mom was out he came over. I was still asleep when he entered. He woke me up to a surprise that made me forget my worries for some time. He changed my room and I had no idea when. There were lanterns in my room that hung from the wall. Balloons all over. Pink, purple, blue. My favourite cupcakes and macaroons were placed on my side table. I was delighted. He knew everything that made me happy. There was a new bulletin board that I went up to. It was stuck on the wall across the bed. It was filled with my pictures. Pictures of my happy days, where I was smiling and laughing. He made post-its for me and stuck them under the pictures. I plucked out a few to see what he wrote in his ant-like messy writing. They were reasons why he adored me. One of it said I was beautiful, another said I was perfectly imperfect. I giggled at that. My eyes were filled with tears and all he did was look right through them. I felt so beautiful. I turned around and he had arranged my favourite breakfast for me, scrambled eggs and waffles. I was amazed. Looking at the balloons and candles all around I wept like a small child. He smiled and came closer. He held me from my waist and made me sit down.

"It's okay if you have problems. We all do, maybe I can't solve them but I promise I won't let you face them alone".

I hid into his trunk and let out the few tears I was holding back. He lifted my face and wiped my tears. He kissed me on my cheeks and placed me back where I was. Protected in his arms. He just let me cry.

I couldn't describe to myself what this was. Was this love? I certainly knew he was way more and I never wanted to lose him. He was not just a friend. He was family.

****

My sleep routine was zeroed down to hell during those days and the noise from outside, even after shutting everything, was fanatical. I would constantly ponder upon the bad things that were happening to me, until one night a thought crossed my mind and decided not to leave. My classmate wanted to kidnap me and he said he wanted to make me realize something, so I started joining the dots. There were three of them. He belonged to the third category. No one ever spoke to him. No one knew of him. He had no friends. He was frustrated and maybe way more that I didn't know about but now I was hoping to.

That morning I got up with a jerk, dreaming about having a vague conversation with Arpit alone – the man who tried to kidnap me. I consoled myself that it was a dream until the newspaper headline read "Woodvilla's crime suspects held". Arpit's picture under it. Déjà vu much, I thought to myself. I hoped this was total coincidence. I ran to my mother and told her that I knew it was Arpit who was behind the mask at the shooting. She stopped cooking her stew, turned the gas off and sat down to ask me "why didn't you tell me?"

"I didn't want to tell anyone, I wanted my answers". I said.

"What do you want to do now?" she inquired.

"I still want my answers", I exclaimed. Surprisingly she didn't panic "go get your answers", she encouraged me. Now that's how you treat an eighteen year old, I thought to myself.

I decided to bunk college, called Rehaan and told him I wanted to see Arpit. He said he would take me to the lock up and ask if we could talk to him but he highly doubted if we would be granted permission. Rehaan's father knew the police commissioner and as we know, everything in Mumbai speeded up with influential contacts. I would get to talk to Arpit alone for not more than fifteen minutes. After which a constable would sit for more inquiry. We had to sneak into the station; avoiding the media at all times was a must. If they had the slightest hint of our intentions they would make it that day's breaking news, not to mention the news that they would add on their own.

Rehaan and I went to Gamdevi police station where they were being held. Two other suspects were people I didn't know, but Arpit was caught. I entered the station to find everything dirty. All the policemen spoke in Marathi. Not a word did I understand. The women constable then took me to a lock-up room where Arpit sat facing his back towards us. Rehaan then said to me "you have to do this alone, so I'm going to wait right here keeping an eye on you till you are done". I nodded because I was too terrified to talk. I was extremely nervous at the thought of facing a criminal. I had never been around dangerous people, but I really wanted to know why he did that to me and what he wanted from me. He sat on the floor and turned around when I said "Arpit?" His face had totally changed from what I had seen last. I could not figure how he had lost so much weight since, but I would never forget those scared eyes and how they looked me when I tore his mask. I went forward and sat on the chair that was kept there for me. He was crying softly.

"Hi", scared I began to speak to him.

"What is your problem, why have you come here, go away". He nearly broke down.

"Look, I'm the only person that knows for sure that you have committed this crime, and I could have told the police long back. I want to hear from you, why you did all this?"

"Do you know my name?" he asked

"Yes Arpit", I replied with uttermost perfection.

"Then I guess that's all you know about me", he came closer and looked into my eyes. "You rich kids know nothing, and are insensitive to anything other than what's going on with yourselves in your own small little self-obsessed world. Do you know how we feel because of you? Let me tell you, the word is LEFT OUT". He came directly to the point "We are always treated like we are a pain, we are remarked all the time as though our existence is nothing, and we are bullied because we don't look good and are not some cheer leaders and prom kings and queens. You decide how your life runs, but who gives you the authority to run our lives? We are not what you all think. We are more. You make categories and divide us, behave accordingly and never understand how we feel. College is torture to us. And not only right now but always. Not only to a few students but to a lot. Look into history and see how many such cases have gone unheard, where students feel ashamed of themselves, where students feel suppressed by others. We hide behind our masks and our books for we are scared how we would be attacked next. And the worst is that our problem is not even given any importance because of course, it isn't happening to you'll".

I took some time to sink in his words. I was so bewildered about the pain in his sentences that I couldn't get my eyes off him. I felt sad about how I never noticed this was happening around me; that it affected people to such a great extent. Why I didn't bother to talk to these people? I know we were different but I didn't know they were treated like that. I was always just told to maintain my distance from them because they weren't good enough for me. Maybe that was the problem; I didn't think they were good enough for me. I kept repeating that sentence in my mind so I could realize that maybe I was wrong about this opinion for all this time. I felt guilty and didn't know what to say to him. This was reality that I had never seen, and never even stressed my mind about. Rehaan was correct about how I lived in a sheltered world. I looked down on the dirty broken grey tiles with regret to now avoid looking at him directly and then turned my head towards the ceiling to see the slow fan throwing no air. I wondered how anyone survived without an air conditioner.

"Throughout college I have been bullied, for no fault of mine. Some people would call me names and make nasty comments about me in front of everyone, laugh about my weight and rag me. My weight is because of thyroid and not because of my eating habits, which in particular, made me very angry. They would harass me and most of all instigate me for a reaction, and this is not just my situation. I hated coming to college. I didn't want to study. You have any idea how that feels?" he asked "why would you? You have everything".

"Then one day I got a chance. A chance to take out my anger and frustration on all of you and make you'll feel helpless just like we do. To get back with everyone who thought no end of themselves and think they can get away with doing whatever they pleased".

I got up from my bench and howled inhumanly "so to get back you decide to dress up like a goon, buy a gun and kill people?" Wow! This world has the potential to justify anything wrong with complete conviction". I was angry and sorry for him at the same time, not knowing which emotion came out stronger curbing the other.

Rehaan ran to me when he heard me yell. I stood close to him. "Is he troubling you?" he asked me.

Arpit from the other side spoke in between "This is the problem. You'll are designed to believe that we are always wrong in every situation".

I didn't understand if I should pity him or get angry with him. Rehaan chose to stay with me. The constable from behind said we had five minutes left.

Rehaan now spoke to Arpit calmly "Buddy, we are here to get a few answers and I know exactly what's been happening with you. I perfectly agree with what all you just said. If you tell us the truth right now, I could maybe help you out".

I looked at Rehaan with the realization that he knew of all this and I didn't. But if he did, why would he not speak up or do something about it?

Rehaan went closer to him and extended a look of pity. He kept his hand on his shoulder and said "You can trust me; we are not here to hurt you. We are just like you".

He broke down completely now. "I was frustrated, I didn't want to hurt you, I'm sorry, I didn't want to hurt anyone but I don't come from a very strong family background like you'll. Getting admission to Woodsvilla on merit was a 'dream come true'. I didn't know it was torture in disguise. All that I went through was more than I expected. I thought I would at least have one friend, but I didn't, and I was morally broken. Things became worse with the bullying and my self-confidence was crushed .Then one day a girl came up to me. She said she could help me take revenge and she could make everyone feel helpless like I did. She said I just had to kidnap you for it and scare everyone else. No one would know who I was. She had everything planned. Initially I told her no, and then she offered me 20 lakh rupees to do it. I needed the money. I was extremely vulnerable", he cried.

"Who was this girl?" we said in chorus. Only I spoke angrily and he softly. Rehaan looked at me and told me to keep quiet. So I did.

"She was your twin sister Amaira, but I have no clue why she wanted to do this and for what. I'm sorry", he said as the constable came in and walked us out.

Chapter 7

Who Will Stay?

"I need to meet Amaira right now". I hastily told mom.

"What happened?" she inquired.

"That girl is in trouble. She thinks she can mess with me. Mom, she was the one behind the entire shooting that day at school. She took undue advantage of Arpit, this classmate of mine, and conspired with him to get me. I don't know why, but I need to…I need to get my answers".

She thoughtfully answered me this time, "I don't really think she could have done something like this, she's not a bad person, and Aria remember she's my daughter and your real twin sister".

"You always want to take everyone's side but mine. You just never think I could be right. She didn't care all these years that she was your daughter, I don't know how then you would know if she's good or not, after knowing that she tried to kill me. You should really think and talk". I walked away gnashing my teeth.

Rehaan and I stalked her Facebook profile and found out a lot more about her. She had few friends from New Zealand. All her pictures had her pouting with red lipstick. There was one boy with her in most of her pictures. Her friends were listed as her family members. Relationship status was complicated and alcohol seemed persistent in all her pictures. Now that she had the same face, I couldn't deny she looked good. We got her number from there and decided to text her to meet us at the Taj Starbucks the next day.

She walked in and sat next to me. Everyone seemed to glare at us, probably because we were twins. Even I would have if I saw two same faces. Rehaan insisted that he spoke.

"Amaira, we know you were behind the shooting. Tell us why".

"I don't know what you're talking about", she lied bluntly.

"We have evidence, and we have an eye witness. We just spoke to Arpit. He told us everything, so it would be better if you don't lie". He said strictly.

She excused herself to get her *caramel frappuccino.*

"Do you think she'll tell us the truth?" I asked Rehaan while she was away.

"She doesn't have an option".

She threw herself on the sofa, something I hated about people. I found it manner less to throw yourself on the sofa making everyone else bounce for no reason. Her coffee almost reached the lid, which she didn't care about.

"What will I get if I say the truth?" she asked as though we were the victims.

"You want something in return for telling us why you committed a crime? That's insane. You know you would anyways be thrown in jail when the police find out, and they will".

"This is Mumbai. I can easily get away. You're such a stupid little kid. I have no interest in talking to you", she turned to Rehaan and continued "Do you want to say something or should I leave? You both are wasting my time".

"Firstly, don't talk to my friend like that, and secondly I will see what I can do about it. We will leave if you think it's a waste of your time, but if you think nothing will happen to you, I will make sure it does. Let's go Aria", he went for my hand.

"Okay I'll tell you everything. Sit".

"Five years ago my mother told me about what she did and how she took me away from my biological mother. I didn't seem to know, understand or take it seriously. We lived hand-to-mouth all our lives so when I learnt that my father was among India's richest men, I wanted the money I thought I should have. So I researched everything about you, came here six months back all by myself and found out your school, your hangout joints, your friends and everything about you".

"But why me?" I stared at her.

"We look identical. I wanted to take your place, take your life, take away your wealth and go back to New Zealand". She said

"Are you behind my father's death too?"

Rehaan held my hand firmly at the seriousness of my words

"No", she said. "That was an accident. I went to Arpit when I came to know he was the most frustrated student in college and would take revenge from you and I offered him money. He agreed to kidnap you and that's just what I wanted. I would have lived your life and kept you in hiding. I hired two goons to help me with everything. Things didn't seem to go as planned at the shooting. After they took you to the hiding place they couldn't get you out of it. So they ran for their lives".

After that I learnt that dad died. So I hired a lawyer and came up to you directly. After which there was news everywhere about how dad didn't have any money and was in debt.

"I can't believe how cunning and money minded you are", I snorted.

"You're not in my place to know". She put her cup down and began to leave.

I felt sad for Arpit; I had now began to feel how he had been feeling all this while. If I was secluded and demeaned I would be frustrated and angry too. I began to think of how much he had been through that he could get swayed by a stranger to take revenge from us. I came to terms with him being poor. I didn't know there were poor people around me, let alone in my class. I didn't know how that was, but I assumed he was in need of money if he agreed to do this for such a small ransom.

Next day I received a call from Forever 21. They wanted to see me urgently. I wondered why.

Now that we didn't have a driver, travelling became tough. Forever 21 was far away and after college I had only an hour to reach the office. Cab would take one and a half. I couldn't make such a silly excuse to them. Rehaan suggested I take a train. I would reach in 45 minutes. The time save was tempting but I had never seen a local train in my life. How would I know how to travel in one?

"Learn", he said "you can't live in Mumbai and not travel in a local train at least once".

"Looks who's talking". I smiled at him.

I decided to go. It would save money too. Had to think about that since pocket money reduced to almost nothing. The station entrance I saw was full of activity. People ran inside like they had missed fifteen minutes of a movie show. I stood in line to buy a first-class ticket as Rehaan had guided me and there again were obnoxious people around who stared at me continuously. So by now I had learnt a trick, I looked at them back with even dirtier looks until they looked down, which they always did. My trick wasn't 100 percent effective here because there were too many people. I couldn't waste my time here doing this. After getting out of the tacky area I went to platform 1 and stood. The train came and women turned crazy. The train stopped for a considerable amount of time for everyone to get in and get out but the highly impatient women wanted to get in all together within the first five seconds, explaining the chaos. I got in when the massacre stopped. I covered my nose with my scarf inside. It was literally stinking like garbage mixed with urine. The women in the compartment were all at ease. They chatted about movies and what was going on in their houses. I couldn't wait for my stop to arrive, but then again, leaving the train for the station was a task. The women made it easier, I didn't have to do anything, they pushed me outside and took me with them. I swirled out of the station like a tornado and never wanted to be back. This was terrible. I wondered how lakhs of people travelled by local trains every single day of their lives. I felt bad for them. I took a moment to realize how blessed I was. Reality kept striking me. This was how life was. Everyone didn't have cars and drivers and still didn't crib about their lives. I felt pain in my heart. The same that I felt for Arpit. It was a sad empathetic pain.

****

My spreadsheets and all of my designs on paper were spread across the round table at the conference room in Forever 21's office. I looked at them and then all the men in blazers quiet surprisingly.

"Any issues?" I began.

"This is the issue". One of them pointed towards my designs. "These aren't good and they are not up to the mark".

I looked at my designs closely while he spoke.

"Some of your designs are incomplete and we asked you for a set of 53. You haven't reached your mark".

"Yes, but I'm sure you know of my family issues and the amount of pressure on me. I have been working as hard as I can in spite of it and would appreciate your patience".

"Yes, we are aware of all your problems and we are very sorry to hear about your loss but this is a huge company and we do not work unprofessionally. Work is work. I'm sorry to let you know but we have decided that we are no longer continuing this line, and I'm sure you know about how the media has now began negative publicity after your father's death. We clearly mentioned to you that girls would be interested in your line also because of your family name and status but I'm afraid negative publicity will affect our company too. We are really sorry but this is nothing personal".

I had tears in my eyes in front of three adult men and one young woman. This time I didn't feel like getting back at them or being blunt to them or even asking them for answers that were, at that moment, going on in my mind. I quietly collected my work that was spread on the table in front of me and put it in my bag and ran out of the building dramatically.

My heart could only now feel pain to a certain extent. The pain beyond was now getting converted into emotions of anger, frustration and dissatisfaction. To top it all was this tool called the cell phone. The generation that used cell phones for every activity of daily life. Which train came when, which movie show at which theatre was most feasible, how to reach a certain location, everything was now on our fingertip. Internet now became a platform to express those unheard emotions that build inside, those feelings that didn't have a platform and those hurdles no one ever heard of. And for me this was all positive until these ratchet days. Facebook or twitter or instagram or snapchat. These personal sharing accounts were no longer personal from the day I started to work with Forever 21. I enjoyed every bit of attention gained through these apps through my days of glorified success. Little did I know what nasty turn they could take for me.

Forever 21 too became public, and not everyone was supportive of it.

It was eight in the evening. I sat down reading my favourite book by Anne Frank when Rehaan called. "What is wrong with you?"

"Huh, what happened?" I asked

"You told everyone that you and I are dating?"

"NO!"

"Okay forget that and explain to me how everyone knows that I was adopted?"

"Who said you are? Who knows? How do they know?"

"Exactly that's what I'm asking you. It's all over social media. You were the only person I had told this to. I can't believe how you could sabotage my image along with yours. You know I'm a private person and I disapprove of anything social. Don't call me again". He hung up.

I logged into all my accounts hurriedly to see what new mess this was. After everything that happened I had completely stopped using social media. Facebook had posts all over about how Rehaan was my friend and adopted. I wondered how anyone knew because I did not remember telling anyone about it. I looked at my instagram comments and was heartbroken. There were images and quotes about me and Rehaan as a couple and then even us breaking up. This was so dramatic. I couldn't believe how so many people had all the time in the world to interfere in my life and then spread rumours about me and him. There were new accounts made for these and I couldn't trace who may have started all this. I now had nobody to even call and talk to about it. So I cried to myself thinking about how I may lose the only friend that I have. Or maybe had. The comments section on my facebook fan page was filled with hate comments. A few of them read. "What do you think of yourself loser! Snobbish bitch!" "You're so ugly that Forever 21 threw you out", "you're good for nothing and your clothes suck", "did you kill your dad for money", "you lie about your relationships and everyone hates you". I think the last one was someone from my school. I read these with an extremely heavy heart. I couldn't hold my tears back and I was sick of it. I didn't understand how someone could not know me personally and make such remarks about me. These people think they could sit behind a screen and write whatever they felt like because nothing would happen to them. It was so utterly mean and cruel of them. I only wanted to talk to Rehaan about all of this. I was broken.

He disconnected my call. Over 5 times. I thought I would give him some time and he would be fine. And then ... he had deleted me from my snap chat. So I went on my facebook. He had deleted me from there too. By now my hands were shivering and I had no clue what to do. I threw the phone in anger. I shut all the doors to my room, switched off the lights, lay in my bed with my blanket and fell asleep crying.

It was so easy in this trap of social being to ignore someone. Facing problems and issues were now old school. One click of a button and someone could be completely out of your life. Demeaned in ways no one would accept. Hurting someone could not have been easier, and there I was helpless as I could be to do anything to get his attention. It frustrated me more at the thought that he could avoid me by deleting me so

I started contacting him even more. Then he took it a step forward. He blocked me from everywhere.

Days passed by and he never answered. And why would he. I shared his deepest secrets with the world. A world that incorporated evil. I just wanted to talk to him and apologize. Do something to get him back, anyhow. Hate comments still caved in. I decided to delete my facebook fan page and my twitter account. I didn't want to face this anymore. I never went to college in the fear of the world mocking at me and just lay in bed all day crying or hugging mom. I tried to keep all of it away from her because she had already been through so much and I didn't want to increase her worries. She only read what was in the papers. She didn't know about what was going on in the social media.

I gave up on life and living. I didn't feel like doing anything anymore. I didn't like food, I didn't like going out, I didn't like seeing anyone and I just wanted to be alone. I wondered how Rehaan wasn't bothered about anything I was going through. He was on my mind all day. I always hoped and wished he would come back in my life. I couldn't stalk him anymore. He had blocked me from whatsapp and all other ways I could contact him.

And then one fine day to make matters worse, I got a message. It was from Priyana Jha. She wrote that she knew Rehaan was adopted because her family was related to his family and she had told everyone about it. I called her.

"Why did you do this?" I shouted.

"To teach you a lesson".

"Lesson? Are you crazy you bitch? I fucking helped you and this is what you do?" I was angry and out of my mind.

"I never needed your help; I wanted to teach you a lesson. You thought no end of yourself and you thought that everything goes on the way you want. This world is not your fairy tale and good people don't survive here".

One more lesson learnt. Do not trust anyone and if you do, don't mistakenly help them.

Then one day thoughts overpowered my brains. Seeped deep down into my soul. Maybe I really wasn't good enough. Maybe I wasn't really meant to be. This wasn't meant to be. I wasn't smart like everyone else and I didn't belong to this world. How I lived was the life I deserved. I was selfish. I was stupid and dumb and unworthy of anything I had. How then, would there be any point to this life, except to bother others. Maybe I was good for nothing. Everyone believed that. I didn't have any friends because I didn't deserve them. I was worthless. I was a pain. And I repeated these words in my head for as long as the words made me believe I had nothing left.

Between the wooden frame of the window on the freshly mist painted wall I saw the dangling yellow light of the sparkling sun peep inside and call me. Maybe it was time. Maybe it was a sign. I smiled.

Chapter 8

A Peek into Real Life

Sometimes there's no hope left, sometimes there's no faith. Our hearts are empty and our hearts are filled. We doubt ourselves and we doubt others. We doubt our existence and we doubt our will. We look for the means. We look for the way. We look for sense in a senseless way. Every door closed, every place is shut. The void spaces enlarge and our path is blurred. We wonder where to go, we wonder where it would take us, we wonder what worse could happen and wonder why we reached here. We either take the right way or the wrong. We either see the light or the dark. And sometimes the darkness hides the light. Sometimes we don't see the light that may have been *hidden* by the dark.

I knew what I was doing was not right. I also knew I wanted to. I took the wrong way. I saw the dark. I thought it'll hide me – for good.

My eyes still hazily looked around trying to make sense of the atmosphere until I decided to close them again. Didn't last long. My ear drums were being drummed by drummers. My eyes were being poked by a knife. I couldn't feel the left side of my body and my right hand felt as though dumbbells were placed on them.

I closed my eyes again. Maybe thought of some peace.

Woke up again. Eyes and face sore and heavy. Didn't know what to do. Closed them again.

I was probably trying to run again. But something was bringing me back.

Breach Candy hospital it was, again. This time I was the patient. I woke up after two days with an all injured body lying in a surrounding that had but, the different shades of blue. The turquoise blue shade of the sky through the window. The finely painted navy blue wall. The denim cloth over all the tables, the navy blue curtains.

I had not a word to respond to humans when I saw them in the room. The doctors mentioned I needed rest, mentally. So I slept and hardly woke up the next two days still confused about my actions and the turn it took. The media, that I hated now, stood outside and asked everyone that came in about what had happened. There were surgical tapes all over my leg and head plastered tight enough for me to feel it and lose enough for it to not hurt. I changed into a pair of jeans after 6 days and was taken outside. I could see the door; I could see a way out. My body had no sensation but I had to try to get back on my feet, still trying to question whether I really wanted to. Not yet maybe. Maybe not.

Rehaan sat in the waiting room. His head bent down looking at his feet until he heard me. 'Hey', I tried to bring out the happiness that ran inside me looking at him. He ran towards me and hugged me. My mom right next to me made it partly weird for the first time. His eyes were puffy and red like he hadn't slept in days. After all the trouble, at least something gave me a slight ray of happiness. Maybe he was not mad at me anymore. Maybe he wanted to be my friend again. Maybe everything would be fine again.

We live on *maybes* all our lives. The faith that things will happen. That they would. We believe in a better tomorrow irrespective of the hurdles of today. We trust people that don't deserve it. We help people that doubt it. We assist people that ignore it and love people that don't validate it. But how often can we deny that those are the only times we think we really live?

I was put in the car and taken home. Rehaan, without a word, was always next to me. I was still overflowing with negativity. I still didn't wish to live and things would be worse now that I survived. I would have to live with it. The media was told that I fell. They speculated, obviously, but that was not our concern. The next day my mom came up to me with the talk I seemed to avoid the most since the incident.

"What is the matter Aria? Can't you handle just a little bit of problem? A little bit of ups and downs in your life. Have I brought you up to be that weak? I understand you are going through a lot but you have to be strong. Didn't you think once what would happen to me if I lost you? How I would survive without you or live with the fact that you were weak and gave up and I couldn't do anything to help".

I didn't say a word. I looked away. She left the room when I reminded her how the doctor told us about the rest, mentally. I didn't want this right now. I was sad that she thought this way. I never actually thought of what would happen to her. It struck me when she cried while asking me those questions.

I woke up to Rehaan next to me. He looked towards the same window I jumped from. I didn't talk to him. Looking at him was bliss. He wore his favourite red Hackett T-shirt and held roses and chocolate bars in his hand, his back straight against the back of the bed with his legs stretched out. He evidently had not shaved in weeks. His hair was long and messy. He turned towards me, found me awake and lay next to me silently. He took my hand and pressed it on his stomach. His fidgeting nature acted upon his rubbing my hands, or maybe that's what I thought. "I'm sorry. I came to know about Priyana. After she heard of this she told me the truth, it wasn't your fault, I'm so sorry".

I let out a sigh of relief.

"Can I ask you something?" I said

"Of course".

"You said you would never leave me, why did you? How could you?"

"Aria, if I didn't leave your hand, how would you learn to walk?"

I rolled over to him and found some long lost solace in his arms.

"You became so attached to me that you forgot yourself. You became excessively dependent and I couldn't see that. You needed me in everything you did and I always am there for you but I wanted you to be able to live without me so that you find your own space and happiness, so that you are independent and so you can face this world alone. I'm here and I will not leave you. Just promise me what you have to do yourself, you will do. You're going to stand up on your feet and we are going to fix this together".

"Rehaan, thank you".

We opened the box of chocolates and I nibbled on them.

****

He wore white – a white long kurta and a turban-like head gear on his empty skull. His smile was that of an angel of god. His eyes were glowing. He had the simplicity of a common man and the spark of an eternal entity. He had not aged a single day since I last saw him. I had never seen him as happy. I stood across him, the center table in the middle. "I love you Aria". "I love you too dad", I responded.

"I want to show you something, come with me".

I walked behind him like a thief behind a cop. Straight in a line listening to his commands with utter perfection. We walked miles and miles. I was tired by now but I would never complain. Every minute I had with him was surreal. We walked further. Further into a negated space. He took me into the darkness. I could see nothing around. Like I was blinded. Voices mumbled and slowly grew louder. The place was scary as could be. I didn't want to walk any further but gathered hope because he was there, right in front of me, my father. I couldn't afford to lose him again. I looked at my feet and finally saw the street under it. A street that led to houses, but not ordinary houses. The houses of the less fortunate.

Small wooden huts; almost joint to each other were called 'houses' by my father. I wondered what we were doing here and why he got me here. One small hut had at least one family living in it; some of them had two. The one we got close to comprised a couple and four to five small children playing in and out. I peeked inside. A small 1970s television set and few kitchen utensils were all I could recognize. I didn't quite apprehend what the rest was. Ragged clothes were hanging in the middle of this hut right on top of their heads. There was only one room. The kitchen from the bedroom had no division, only a small broken door demarked the washroom. There was no bedroom. They slept on the floor. I frowned, still wondering what I was doing here. A small dirty gutter with black water flew right outside these joint huts.

A few steps ahead was a double storey hut with a broken ladder going up. This little place was even smaller.

"These are not even beggars, they work for a living. Most of them are servants in the houses of the rich or work as labourers in factories. Even those you see there", he pointed towards the children "work for a living".

My frowning face had now turned into a straight face and my little heart ached as I looked at the huts as I advanced. He took me ahead to a small family of a man who lived with his wife and three children, all of whom wore ragged mixed colour clothes. Black with red and yellow with green combinations all patched onto one another. Their clothes were dirty. I see they had no washing machine. I wondered where they even washed their clothes. How could anybody live like this?

"They do, they have no choice", answered my dad while I wondered how he heard the voice in my head.

The outside of their hut was their working place. They made pots for a living. Clay, mud and sand were turned into the shape of their choice with excessive heat implied on it. Their pottery machine was intricate. The hands were dirty with the clay as they shaped them into piggy banks which they called *gullaks*. One of their sons would take the semi-dry pot upstairs to dry them in the sun. They made all different shapes, some for flower pots, some round like plates and others were just big empty pots for storing water and keeping it cool for houses that didn't have refrigerators. This was new to me again. I never thought of how one could live without a refrigerator because I never thought someone couldn't have it. I had to go back and remind myself of how old I was to not know all this. I stared at the pots and asked them how much one was for. The women smiled at me as if I was buying all of them.

"ye bees rupe ka hai".

"Rs 20 for the *gullak*", she said. I turned to the woman and turned back at the pots and then to the family.

"You see them Aria?" my dad spoke "Someone out there is happy with less than what you have". I had read that on a tumbler somewhere, never paying much attention to the meaning. Not knowing it could mean so much more than what my small brain could imply of it.

I woke up panting, remembering the dream so precisely for the first time that it didn't seem to be a dream. Retaining information about dreams when I got up was the first thing I did after waking up to them.

Why would my father take me to slums? Why would I get such a dream? I thought dreams could only have things we know about and have seen before. This was shocking to me. I had never before seen slums, neither had I seen what poverty was. Maybe my father actually wanted to tell me something. Maybe he was showing me things I should see. I recollected the entire dream once again still lying down on my bed out of breath trying to make sense of it. There were poor people out there. Nothing of what I imagined them to be. They had so little, almost nothing. They were born in poverty, lived in poverty and died in even more poverty. He said these were not beggars. These were hard working poor people who had nothing for a living only because they were born that way, unlike me who was born with luxuries. Maybe they were no less than me, maybe no more than me. They were born a certain way and I was born a certain way. Only one thing I couldn't help but register into my mind forever – these people had so little and were yet happy!. They had no cars, no ac bedrooms, no education, something that was basic necessity, but their smiles were larger than the ones who did. They had never seen the world, they knew they were poor, they knew they had problems but they were content. They didn't want more money, they didn't want a bigger house, they didn't want lavish clothes and footwear and maybe that was the reason they were happy. Maybe this world I lived in made me the way I was. Made me greedy and materialistic. Made all of us like that. Made me want more and not be happy with whatever I had. Made me compete to make me survive.

The children were so happy, hitting a tennis ball with a badminton racket. Maybe they didn't know how it worked and that's the reason they were happy.

They were joyful because they didn't cry to have a shuttle cock for a badminton racket or a tennis ball for a tennis racket. They didn't know how to play; they didn't have any rules, any boundaries. They were happy because they could play. Play with whatever they had, moreover with whoever they had. All kids played together. No one was differentiated, no one was kept aloof or had to live up to standards to play their games or to fit in.

I remembered college.

College divisions.

Remembered Kiara.

Then Jay and Rahil.

The bullies.

And then the difference.

I jumped out of bed and got ready, my heart still feeling a certain pain from realization. I packed all of my old clothes that I didn't use and put them into a huge cardboard box. I took a cab to Child Care India and asked to see the head. I handed over my box to the NGO and asked if I could help monetarily. They said they would happily accept whatever I could offer. While leaving the NGO of orphaned children, an old man dressed in a suit, wrinkles all over his face made a comment without my notice "You don't find redemption in material, you find them in your deeds".

"And you mean to say?" I asked.

He walked away not answering. I was tired of people not giving me answers and saying things to me that had the "inside" meaning.

Mom was very proud of me. I told her about the dream and she said that dad is always with me and through this dream he taught me something he couldn't teach me in his life and that I should value and understand it.

"We always thought we had enough time to teach you about life and let you enjoy till you grew up but we should have implemented better values into you since you were young. Dad always regretted that he didn't have as much time for you during your growing up days. He was so busy building his empire that he forgot the real empire to build is you. You can never tell what destiny has in store for you".

I told her about the old man I met in the NGO while I was leaving and she explained to me what he meant.

"He was trying to tell you that giving your stuff was a very noble deed but if you really want to make a change in you and in others then you need to do more than that. You need to help them by empathizing with them, knowing them and their problems and offering solutions".

"What should I do mom?"

"Maybe you should join an NGO and help

people. But before that, if there's anger in your heart about things, read this article".

She handed me the newspaper article, by a young writer Aleena Qureshi, that explained how anger should be used in the correct form, manner and direction.

****

I was ardent on doing something. Doing something no one ever thought I would. I wanted to see change, and for that I wanted to be the change. I wanted to see more of this life that I most evidently evaded most of my life. I looked up various NGOs and their activities and called a few of them. They were all looking for volunteers. I wanted to do something more impactful than just teaching children. WAD was an NGO that excited me the most. They dealt with problems of women and problems of people who were addicted to alcohol or drugs. It seemed very hardcore and depressing at first but I thought this is what I needed. They told me to come and take a look.

It was an old building and I had to climb four floors. There were strange people all around walking up and down as I climbed. The office was where they wanted to see me. It was small and unkempt. The lady official of the NGO asked me why I wanted to do this. She knew of me, thanks to my family name; I wondered if that was a curse or boon now.

"I want to help people", that's all I said and that was truly all I came here for. She told me they would train me for six days for counselling and then take a test to find out if I could be placed in their counselling cell. I thought it would be pretty cool. I began training at their main NGO centre which was way better than the office. They even had shelters for women who didn't have houses and were in genuine need of them.

This wasn't professional training, therefore some basics taught at the NGO were

Positivity ... at all times you must be and teach your patient that positivity is what changes perspectives and situations.

Looking from a different point of view ... many vigilant and stubborn souls would be thrown your way. The only way to deal with them is to make them look at things from the view of happiness and intellect.

Being strong ... no matter what they have been through, they are not your family. You have to sympathize with them and not empathize. There is no problem that cannot be solved. You have to deal with them strongly and help them find their way, and in no way, break down in front of them or feel bad about their situations.

Listen ... the highlights of every day was how to listen, carefully and patiently. Half of the problems of the patients were solved because they let out what they held inside of them that they couldn't share with anyone.

Be unbiased ... behaviours and problems of patients were to be accessed and not judged. Every action of theirs had a reason behind it.

I passed the test with the caution that I had to be strong. They even mentioned that I may have a problem because of my broken Hindi and the accent that came with it. They analyzed that I had a weak heart but gave me the opportunity looking at my enthusiasm. Two hours thrice a day I spent with complete strangers of all different ages. It went smoothly the first few weeks. I almost thought that the patients only needed to talk and let go off things.

One woman around the age of thirty six had been going through domestic violence. She was being beaten up every day by her alcoholic husband and violent in-laws. She didn't have the strength to tell anyone about it or leave him. I was amazed at the tolerance power of the woman. She still wanted to stay and help her husband. I would have shot the man.

"What do you really want to do?"

"Mujhey khush rehna hai". She was tired of being sad; she just wanted to be happy.

"Aapko strong rehna padega".

Children today were born into English language and when we spoke in Hindi it was always combined with English words – thus the origin of *hinglish*. After an hour long discussion she thanked me and said she would talk to him and give it a last chance until her next meeting with me.

I was called for hearing in Arpit's case. My life was getting more tragic day by day. How many twenty-year olds would have been called to a court for a hearing I wondered? Law is something no one could evade. I had to go. Weeks into the shooting and after much searching the police collected every item found in the school that day. They sealed them and asked every one of their belongings. A ton of different things were found. The alarming massacre that made everyone run inanely, lost items from a lot of students in the mess. Bracelets, wallets, watches were found and held. The owners of these were called and questioned if the items belonged to them. I remember going to the cops. I didn't understand why they would call me. If I was the victim how could I be the culprit? Apparently Tanya, who I had lent my scarf that day, had left it in the D hall. It was found by the investigators and I was called for questioning along with Tanya. She said that she had borrowed it from me and left it there when everyone ran to leave after the black men had left. I thanked them for giving me my horribly expensive scarf back and letting me out, but they did not leave Tanya. I looked at the policeman who stared at Tanya. I think she was in trouble, but I learned later that they found her to be innocent.

Arpit's locket was left there. He was called too. The police found it in the small room that they had taken me to. Not only his locket but his clothes were identified too. No one had any idea about what his clothes were doing there. He wasn't revealing anything.

At the trial Arpit was held by policemen and taken in front of the judge. I sat on the long wooden bench next to my mother. They made him take oath on the Gita. Asked him a few questions I didn't pay attention to. I was wondering what I should do. I was called to the witness box.

"Do you recognize this man, young lady?" the lawyer asked

"Yes I do. He studies in my class".

"How well do you know him?"

"Not very well".

"But you say he's in your class".

"That does not mean he's a friend. I know nothing about him. I have never had a conversation with him. I have just seen him".

"Interesting for classmates", he remarked. "Did you see him at the day of your prom?"

"No". I said

"Do you, under any circumstances feel that he could have been behind the shooting at your school the other day?"

"I don't think so".

I lied and lied enough to feel awfully guilty but I did not want him to go to jail. I heard what he said to me and realized his intentions were not bad. His circumstances were. I wanted to help him whichever way I could. My mom, who knew I was lying, held my hand as I sat on the bench and reassured me that my decision was correct. Forgiveness was hard but peaceful.

Arpit was released that day due to lack of evidence. I met him the next day.

We walked towards the school, without a word. He didn't have much to say to me, out of guilt I supposed. I didn't know what to talk to him either. Silence shadowed all throughout school until we reached the hallway. I had avoided going to the hallway since the shooting. He told me he wanted to show me something.

"You know I'm an orphan", he randomly spoke as we walked.

"Really?"

"Yeah".

"Sorry, I didn't know".

"It's okay".

"Who do you live with?" I asked.

"Rats mostly".

I turned to him "Haha very funny!"

"You remember the place you unmasked me? That dirty little small place?"

"Yaa...about that, I had to ask you, how were your clothes found there by the police?"

"Because that's where I live".

Chapter 9

Eradication of Fear

"You don't have a house?"

"Actually I do, but I don't like living there".

"Where? With whom?"

"I used to live with my foster parents. They adopted me when I was small from the orphanage, Child Care India".

Arpit was homeless. He was not a criminal. He was adopted but he was just like us. I realized he was once among the kids I saw at Child Care India where I went to donate. It was sad. I was seeing too much pain these days but I wouldn't deny the fact that it was teaching me a lot. We all are born a certain way and live our lives in the comfort of that zone but lately I have been realizing that if you really want to expand your learning process, comfort zone isn't the place. It's important to get out of it and learn through the experiences of others. We are all different from one another but what unites us are our struggles we face. One could have more than the other, someone could be stronger than the other, but we build our learning process by living on the experiences of others. I was learning and accepting life by now understanding that life was more than what I saw and if I wanted to grow I needed to stop criticizing and judging people on where they came from and accept them for who they are and what they have done while going through what seems frankly impossible for me.

"Why don't you live with your foster parents?"

"I don't like them. They are always fighting with each other. They don't have children and they are least bothered about me. To escape from the problems there, I sleep here at night most of the times. They stopped giving me money after I had a huge spat with them at home one day. I told them I didn't want their money or favours. That's how I got swayed when Amaira offered me money".

How someone could live alone, without their parents, surviving this harsh world all by themselves. I wonder how they learnt the things that our parents taught us. They had no one to teach them the basic values and etiquettes we grow up with. He sounded more sensible than me. He knew more than me, mostly which was because he was out there in this world all by himself. No one was sheltering and taking care of him. That dirty little place had been home for him for quiet sometime, a place no one even knew about. He sneaked into it every night, but since the shooting day the place was under tight security.

"Where did you live after the shooting day?" I asked curiously as I looked deeper into his 'room'.

"Don't worry it's not that dramatic also. I went back home and lived with those strangers".

We both giggled in the hallway, our voices echoing enough to make us realize we should leave.

I liked Arpit, he was not a bad person, just a troubled one. I decided I would remain friends with him and not differentiate anymore. I was glad about the decision I took to save him.

Aleena's next article was not an article, it was a poem. Never missed her writing since the day my mom introduced me to it. The poem was on life and struggles. It read

Into this world I came
Nothing knew about this tame
As easy and swift as it looks
The seriousness of contrary cooks

From toddling to walking
Turns into worldly talking
The immense joy of childhood
Into the responsibilities life took

The craving for accomplished knowledge
Teaches the clarity of being polished
Taking into a roller coaster
To know the hardships of being fostered

At every step we realize
How life creates its surprise
To know it's not easy to live
But every moment is worthwhile in it.

****

"What are you scared of?" Rehaan asked me suddenly as we walked up the staircase to his room in the duplex.

"Haha what kind of a question is that"?

"Say na".

"But why?"

"Just..."

"I've to tell you something, there's this writer called Aleena. She writes columns in the newspaper. Mom showed her writings to me. I really like them. I wish I could meet her someday. She's so inspirational, you should read her work too".

"I shall", he handed me a piece of paper and a pen.

"What's this for?"

"Take this. Write down everything you are scared of".

"Huh? What...What, but why?" I asked.

"Just think, and write it down. Stop asking me questions".

I looked at the paper for a good 10 minutes. He went out to get something. I don't know what he was trying to do. I stared deeper into the paper. I thought to myself. What was I scared of. Then I wrote something.

Running a race.

That was what I was scared of. Then thoughts and fears of the past relapsed in my mind.

Something I really wanted to do and was scared of was work, which included making clothes, opening a brand and to become something. I would never try doing that again. I wasn't meant for it. I wasn't smart enough for it.

Then I wrote the media. I was terribly scared of the media and how they had portrayed me and how they could use their power to deteriorate a person's character and dignity.

Of being poor. The fourth thing I wrote down and smiled to myself.

Of losing people...

Of animals.

I hated animals.

The pen was in my mouth as I thought to myself what else I was scared of. Rehaan walked in with his remote for the ps4. He plugged in the controllers and started the game. Asked me to play. I laughed. He knew I didn't know how to.

"Try", he said.

"But I can't at all. I'm extremely technologically challenged and you know that".

He grinned, "There's nothing you can't do, you just don't wish to do it".

"Such a lazy bum you are", he made a face at me, which ended in an angry pillow fight that messed the entire room.

He took the piece of paper from me and slipped it into the pocket of his jeans. I didn't expect what was in store for me the next day. The small piece of paper took away a lot. For good.

Tracks. People. Noises. Cheering. Medals. Everything that I was scared of. All together.

I wanted to run back away from here, from this crowded ground. I held Rehaan's hand, made a small face and begged him to turn around and for me to leave. He held my hand firmly without letting it move. He was stronger. It was the interschool competition for Santun School and I had no clue what we were doing here. We weren't in school and far away from being a part of this in any way.

"You'll run here today".

"What?? Are you insane Rehaan? I'm not. Let's go, please".

"Will you just trust me?"

"I do, but I can't to do this". I was almost very angry now.

"And that's why I want you to. The only time we can live is the time without fear". He paused "and you my love, have too much of it. It needs to go".

"You have no idea about anything Rehaan", I put his hand away from mine. "You don't know what I've faced with athletics and running".

"I don't even want to. I want you to run so that you can put it behind you".

I looked into his eyes in the middle of the tracks in the field. Suddenly all the people and the cheering and the noises dimmed out. There was silence. He just looked at me. Deeply. Lovingly. Respectfully. Just him and me, standing under the sparkling sunlight.

He believed in me and I didn't. I thought that was reason enough for me to try this. I wasn't a very rebellious person and could never be one with him. I just couldn't get myself to argue or say "No" to him. The look in his eyes made me weak enough to do as he said.

"Where do I go?" I asked him.

"I've spoken to the principal, you've to go stand in the lane I tell you in a while".

We stood in the stands, looking at other races. 100 metres, 200 metres and then there was 400 metres. All different grade students one after the other so that there was time for the contestants to rest and prepare. I looked at Rehaan. He was happily cheering away for the contestants. There were two sides to him. He was the guy that didn't care much about the world and what it thought of him. Many called him practical. He was funny at the same time. I saw him differently. For me that practical part was on the other side of the wall that protected and sheltered his soft heart. He was helpful and kind and generous but he always wanted himself to be seen as strong. Wanted to look all brave from the outside to the world, the tough guy who doesn't cry…but inside he was the guy who cared more about people, the guy who spoke up for others when he had to take a stand and the guy for whom loyalty and respect for others came before what the world thought of him. He probably didn't care about the world, but he cared about his close ones.

I don't know why guys had to pretend to be strong and brave. Probably two sides of the same coin. It was okay to be soft hearted and caring. He was just so.

I stood in the lane next to the students from the 10th grade. I remember when I was one of them. That frightful day made me realize what fear was and what it could do. It was the interschool race even back then. I was the fastest runner in school and everyone knew I would make my school proud. But unluckily things didn't go as planned that day. I realized I had lost practice. When I ran, I ran as fast as I could. The fastest I could. But I saw people running faster than me. So while the race was going on, I looked at them.

Something I shouldn't have done. When I looked to the right and saw Priya run faster than me, I got scared. I got so scared that I became slow. Slower than her. That held me down. I reached the line after her. But that was not all. I reached after her and two more people. I was not even in the top 3. I let down everyone and never ran again. After that day I could never run. I never had the courage to run. I always felt like that would happen to me again. All the time. And that I would have to carry the burden of letting everyone down every time I ran. That day's fear was stuck to me even till today.

While I was still in the thoughts of the past, I heard Rehaan speak "There's no winning and there's no losing. You are here to face your fear. So do it because you like it. Do it because it gives you a reason. It'll only be possible if you don't look at who's next to you and whether they are better than you or not. Just work on how to be better yourself. That will make you a winner even if you don't win".

And so I stood with everyone in the line and started to run at the gun shot like there was nobody looking. I almost ran with my eyes closed. Fear suddenly vanished and I felt like I let go of a pain that was within me without me knowing about it. I had not run since the 10th grade but what I knew was this was something I liked doing. I thought about all the times that I won and how happy that made me. I stopped thinking about the one time I failed because I realized that the only time we fail is when we give up instead of getting up again. I opened my eyes. We had all crossed the line but I didn't know who came first and who came last. Because for the first time, it didn't matter.

****

I took Rehaan to my NGO one day. I wanted to show him around. I couldn't imagine doing anything without him being a part of it. I wanted to show him my patients and how nice they were. I wanted to show him this little girl I met at the shelter, her parents had abandoned her when she was 2 years old and she didn't have anywhere to go. Somebody found her and left her here at the shelter. She was my friend now. Strange for someone like me that didn't even make friends with classmates. But I was a different person now – still negative but hopefully a humble one.

Rehaan met Ayushi, which was her name at the shelter, not her real one though. Didn't matter. She liked it.

He looked at her with those innocent eyes. He was so generous in his behaviour towards her. Took out a chocolate from his laptop bag and gave her. He asked her what she likes. He hung around with her and even played her favourite game with her – hop scotch. She called it *langdi*. I took out my camera and took a picture of the amazingly happy scene I could cherish forever.

This happiness was different from the happiness of buying clothes. Different from buying heels and bags. This was the happiness that came from inside the heart without having anything to pay for. Maybe my idea of happiness had always been incorrect. This was the happiness money could never buy me. This happiness was happiness in someone else's happiness.

The woman Gita came back; I was to counsel her today again. Rehaan sat outside in the glass box with the supervisors. They could hear what we spoke. They always had to check if I was doing my job correctly and incase anything went wrong. She wore a turquoise saree. Cleaner than all the previous ones I had seen her wearing. It was ironed well today with the white boarder under the black lace. Nice mix of combination I thought. The design took me back to my designing days. How much I loved mixing colours and creating designs.

"Aapki wajah se main aaj zinda hu". I held my breath as she said that.

She said she was alive because of me. She had given up on her life until she decided to come here for help. She continued to tell me that she gained strength talking to me and I was so happy that I could jump but then I controlled my feelings when she became more serious and started crying.

I was bewildered already. She was supposed to be happy.

"Mainey unhe chod diya". She had left her alcoholic husband.

She was extremely sad and cried like a small child in front of me. She said she had nowhere to go. Her name in the society would be spoilt because women were always projected wrong, even if it wasn't her fault. She lived with her mom in a really small house now.

"At least you are not getting beaten up every day anymore. You will soon find your happiness". I assured her and began crying myself.

I just couldn't control it now. My heart was so full that my eyes couldn't help but sync with it.

My supervisor came and stopped the session. He took Gita away because I started crying. I remembered the time I was taught to be strong at all times because being weak would mean I'm not a good counsellor and couldn't handle problems.

My supervisor started yelling. "We should have never given this to you to do. You aren't strong enough".

I understood I had done wrong but I cried even more. Rehaan came into the box and saw me cry. He looked at the supervisor.

"You know she's not as strong as you. She's trying her best and you know that because of what we just heard Gita say".

He was so adorable. He was so nice to me. He always stood up for me. How could someone be so genuine? I started wiping the tears that rolled down my cheeks.

"I know it's not easy to change quickly. She comes from a different place, but the girl that once cried over her Jimmy Choo heels breaking was now crying at the sight of someone's house break. That's a big difference. I'm sure that's a classic example of what you want to show to your patients. Humility and gratitude".

The supervisor left with a straight face and my assistant Sheila came in. She was a sweet middle-aged woman. She took care of everyone in the shelter.

"You know he didn't mean to be rude. But we work in this big organization where we can't afford to make such mistakes. We are already taking a risk by giving you patients. You are a wonderful person and the fact that you want to help people makes us glad. But you have to remember that you are small. You are only 20 years old. You haven't really seen life's greater problems. I would suggest you don't take this up right now and give yourself some more time. When you are more mature to handle this and know people and situations better you can come back and join us. That would then be our honour. Enjoy your life now, you are already doing a lot for this organization by sponsoring children and the needy".

"Thank you so much for your advice. I think you are absolutely correct. She shouldn't be taking so much at this age". Rehaan shook her hand while we prepared to leave. I kept Gita's private cell phone number with me. We weren't allowed to take personal information of the patients so I had to sneak it in.

Chapter 10

The Content Life

"We are now going to make you do what you like doing most, and something I didn't know you were scared of".

I was extremely petrified by Rehaan's statements these days. From making me write my fears on a piece of paper one day, to going on to removing them, I could expect anything from him now. I think he had no other work in life. He was behind my life. All he would ever do is worry about what I want to do and what would be better for me.

"And now what is that?" I asked him.

"You are going to design again".

"Listen Rehaan, go home, you are drunk". I laughed so hard, confounded in my heart about what he was going to say next.

"Why are you so negative about everything? Before hearing me out you want to reject my proposal. Always".

"Sorry, I'm listening tell me".

"You don't need to work under anybody. You don't need someone to tell you that your passion is good for you. Whatever happened with Forever 21 was in a way good for you. You are your own inspiration; there's nothing that will stop you from doing what you want to do because of what others think. I have a plan".

Never had I witnessed an act of such selflessness before, I was even doubting it now. Why would he do so much for me? Why would he ever want to help me so much? Why was my life the center of his life? There was way more he needed to tell me. But the kind of people we were, we kept such things to our hearts. We could never express too many emotions, at least to each other. I thought it was better if it remained that way. It avoided unnecessary problems and we didn't live in the future. What was meant to be would be. So we just enjoyed the moment.

I realized so many people, and so many emotions, were crushed, were mutilated and destroyed only by the thought of what would happen in the future. We give up so much most of the times because of this fear. We give up our today, thinking about the future, not knowing what could have been is the hardest regret you could have. Living in the present and enjoying it is as important as living. So for once, we should lift the veil, unblock the roads, and aim for the sky. Because the happiness that comes with living free is the happiness that's meant to be.

"You have your sketches; you have your imagination for more sketches. Sketch out the clothes you want to design and make them yourself. I know it's a big deal and it's not as easy as Forever 21 laying up your designs at their stores for direct sales but I'm sure starting from scratch would make you learn about the intricate details of the business and give you a stronger hold on the market".

"That's a lot of work, but I want to do it. I know where to get the cloth and all the material. I know where to get it stitched, but I don't have a store, how would I sell it?"

"Well sell it online in the beginning – through online channels, websites, instagram and facebook. If it works out well, we'll design the clothes in bulk and open a store as your brand".

"We don't have that kind of money".

"I will sort that out for you. We will look for investors".

I loved how he always said we instead of you. How he meant that he would always do everything with me. Even though this wasn't his forte.

When I told mom about the whole conversation, her face was glowing for the first time since dad passed away. She was sympathetically more excited than I was. She boosted my confidence even further.

I began sketching, with more passion than before. Over the days a lot of sketches were ready, sooner than I had expected. I was more motivated to do better. This time I had to work harder. I had to prove something to the world. I had to prove something to all those people who thought I was good for nothing. To all those people who said I was something only because of my dad's name. To all those people who bullied me. I could not go out answering them individually; neither could I give it back to Priyana. But what I could do was to get back at them with my work and show them what I was capable of achieving. Something I learnt I should do from Aleena's article about anger seeking direction.

I went around in the shabby areas of Mangaldas, where good cloth was given at cheap rates closest to home and picked up what I thought would best suit my pieces. I then went ahead to pick two different tailors who hardly understood my Hindi and told them exactly how I wanted my dresses and tops and their tailoring. I researched the market and its trends extensively. Their time for tailoring gave me time to organize how I would sell my stuff online.

Amaira suddenly showed up at our flat one day. It was a weird feeling when I had to call my house a flat now instead of a bungalow. How much had I hated her! She walked in through the door with one large suitcase and a cross handbag that hung across her shoulder and rested on her waist. She had put on weight since the last time we saw her. She went up to my mother and spoke.

"I'm sorry for everything mom".

Wow. Now she was calling my mom hers too.

"What I did was wrong. I was jealous that I didn't have her life. Even more jealous that I didn't have you. I'm leaving so you could be happy and live as you did without me".

"Where will you go?" my mom asked her as they both cried.

"From where I came".

My mom wept even more. I started to realize how I behaved towards Amaira was maybe wrong. She was my sister. She was the child of my mother. We shared the same womb. At the same time. As much as my mom would have to ignore the aspect of her that led her here, she did have a soft corner and pain in her heart for the fate of her daughter that she couldn't control. But maybe I could change that.

I looked into her eyes and saw the old me. I saw the transition of me in her. She was materialistic to me. But then so was I till a few months ago. She behaved like any other typical teenager. The look in her eyes made me see how she had changed, the same way that I had. She wasn't taught the same values. She never had a family. She didn't know what those feelings were. I couldn't help but look at it from her side and…forgive her.

"Stay with us, don't go!" I said. I saw my mother smile in surprise. She was glad I said what I did.

"I have to go. I have a mother waiting for me. I cannot leave her. I'll come back".

Amaira left, taking a piece of our hearts like dad had. That was family maybe. That was the strength of blood. Of blood relations.

The designs I put up almost got immediate attention from the masses. Also because of my previously established designing name with Forever 21. Another plus was that the clothes were sold at a more reasonable price, which pooled in more customers.

A company called Sylentrics emailed me. They wanted to set up my work at stores and help me make a brand. They would charge me a small rate from my sales but not interfere with my brand or designs. After reading their contract, I signed up for my own brand and store. Back on my feet I thought to myself. Life wasn't that bad I guess.

I had given up. Something I should have never done. I should have never let a small failure and a few problems overpower the decision of my entire life. We give up so easily not looking at what we could earn if we didn't. I was bullied. And bullied constantly over a really long time. My self-confidence was crushed. I had really low self-esteem. Everyone who I thought would stay had left and I was completely helpless. But if there is anything I could tell my younger self, it would have been "look at how much you are going to achieve, look at where you are going to reach, don't give up. It's all a lesson in disguise".

The media was back in action. This time they were confused what to articulate about me. Because this time it was me who decided how I wanted to be projected. They couldn't but talk well about me. They asked me about my designs. I learnt to give them exactly what they didn't want. I spoke positively, and when they took out my past, I spoke diplomatically, telling them how everyone in life needs to go through something, to become something better. Newspaper and magazine articles about me were extremely fun, with quoted headlines like 'back in action', 'here to stay', 'after fall comes rise' – the last one being my favourite.

I was waking up to surprises every day. This time something I didn't want to really face. Kiara, Jay and Rahil were home. Mom asked if she should let them in. "Of course", I said.

They sat down on the sofa in the hall. Staring at all different places till I got ready and reached the hall. I sat down with them without saying a word. I was mad at Kiara and would never look at her the same way. I didn't even look her in the eye. The bell rang before anyone could say anything. Rehaan came and sat down too.

"We are really sorry", Kiara began.

"We didn't know what to do", Rahil added.

"Of course, such innocent kids you'll are", I taunted. "Even I don't think I know what to do or to say to you'll", and once I began I just had to let out everything.

"You'll call yourself friends? I don't understand how you'll could leave me when I had no one and that too when I needed you'll the most. If you'll could do this to me remember you'll are no good friends to each other too. One problem tomorrow and you'll would leave each other. I never expected this from any of you. And Jay, you've been friends with me for so long. What have we not seen or done together. You, doing this to me? Sidelining me and neglecting me, for no fault of mine. How could you?"

"It's not his fault Aria, he got influenced. Everyone got influenced", Kiara interrupted.

"By whom?"

"By me. By the other college students. Mostly by Priyana. She told us that if we remain friends with you our name would go down like yours and everyone would hate us too. It would reflect on us and on our families".

She was reminding me of what had happened to me and I hated that. I could hardly hold on to my tears.

Rehaan came to me. "We all make mistakes right. You did too. They are genuinely sorry and they regret doing what they did. You should forgive them".

And how can you tell that Rehaan? What makes you think they won't leave me again? Now that my life is all good they have come back again. They will leave me again. I don't trust anyone anymore".

"We won't", Rahil said looking at the floor. "You can trust us", Kiara added.

"I will see. I want to take some time".

"Sure. Of course". We all went for lunch.

****

Life was getting stable. My life was like a huge storm that I thought would never end. Like the rains that would never stop, like the dark that only destroys. But the pain taught me, that the storm clears path for a brighter road ahead. After the rains comes the clear sky with the pretty rainbow and only after its dark will you be able to see light.

Mom sat next to me. She wore a saree today. A bright red one draped around her body and it flew downwards from the shoulder. She was going somewhere I assumed. She had a worried face. I was making sketches and uploading pictures simultaneously.

"Aria, I have something to tell you".

"Yeah Mom".

"Mr. Mirchandani has been successful in recovering the money that your father had in the Swiss Bank account".

"It's a lot?" I asked softly, without knowing what I wanted to hear.

"Not as much to make our lives go back to what it was, but definitely enough to begin where we left things".

"Since when did you know? About this account and money?"

"We knew he had money deposited there, but we were not sure about its revival or whether that was against the loan taken for the mine or not. Mr. Mirchandani looked into everything and finally told me about it yesterday. I think we can have our house back for the time being and repay most of our debts. Mr. Mirchandani and I are looking into the matters ahead, as to how we can start investing the remaining money after repaying the loans".

"That's good news".

"Doesn't sound like you are happy. As happy as you should be".

"Mom, money doesn't matter to me anymore. I've realized money isn't everything. Of course it is important and if I had it I would buy whatever I could, but not beyond what's necessary. Life is way more than what money can buy you. Money doesn't buy you class. Or respect. It doesn't make you above or below anyone. What makes you who you are are your deeds, and your love and affection towards others. And how strong you are. How positively you can handle situations. I've learnt that everyone has ups and downs in life and everyone goes through tough times, but you can't sit and cry over what could have been. Or how much you don't have. You can only be happy when you realize you are blessed with what you have. And how you can make the most of it. Mom those kids at the slums dad took me in my dreams had nothing, and they were yet so happy".

My eyes filled with tears as I tried to remember everything at flashback. How proud I was of everything I had before. And how little that was now. I cried telling mom how I thought others were below me because they had less money than me. I released they were in fact better people than me. How snooty I was. How I thought no end to myself. How I thought I would never have to face any problem. How indifferent I was to the pain of other people. I decided I would change that. And that I would do everything I could for the people who were less privileged and were meant for greatness. I would begin finding talent and placing them on correct platforms.

"Mom you know what. Recently I've begun thinking that through my work and otherwise I find an obligation in myself to help others. Because genuinely, what happened to me was for a reason. It was an eye opener. I find a responsibility in me to help others because that's why God gave me such an experience. If I was born with more money and given a better education that would have been better for someone smarter and less privileged than me, then I was given all of it for a reason. For uplifting those others through the powers vested in me".

Mom was so proud and her hug said it all.

Over the next six months I had prepared myself to be the ultimate reigning queen of designing. My store Flaunt Affairs was the ultimate destination for catering to all fashion needs of every young woman. I worked every day and every hour to make myself the youngest top designer of India. I had collaborations with all major brands and I opened two new stores single handedly in Mumbai. Over the years I wished to open them all over the country. I worked closely with Child Care India and a small amount of my earnings from Flaunt Affairs went for the overall development of the orphaned children.

I met Jay, Rahil and Kiara often. They seemed to be back to normal. Our friendship grew stronger than before. And my love for Rehaan only increased. I only wish he knew. Arpit was welcomed in our group whole-heartedly. He became a part of us without any hesitation, as opposed to what I initially thought.

My biggest happiness was that we shifted back to our bungalow. I wouldn't now mind living at the flat but if I had a chance to move back, I would be happy. The loan against the house was paid off by selling properties and recovering money from foreign bank accounts. Mr. Mirchandani was taking care of the rest. He prepared regular meetings with us to discuss the developments.

I realize change is constant. Change in fact is the steadiest phenomenon that occurs all throughout life whether it is appealing or not. We are resistant to such change and do not readily accept it, making life difficult and problematic. Throughout life we assume everything will be perfect. That we are going to have the same people around us and will be subject to the same situations. But no one ever faced the same problems throughout their lives, no one ever lived happily defiant to change. So we should embrace change that comes with life.

I was turning 21 on the 1st of February. The last time I checked I was sixteen or something, stepping out in the real world after school. I wished to throw a huge party on my birthday. I wanted everyone I knew and everyone I loved to be with me on that day – everyone who had seen my highs and my lows my good and my bad. I prepared way before hand. I planned a theme party at home and decided what food I wanted. If only I knew my whole life would turn around again at a party.

Disney, being my favourite thing under the sun had to be the theme of my party. I loved everything about Disney. I spent hours a day, even at the age of 20, to watch Disney movies and Disney princesses – right from Cinderella to Rapunzel. I decided to dress as my favourite Disney princess, Ariel, minus the mermaid tail of course. I made sure Rehaan would agree to be Eric, and he most happily did. I took the effort to decorate as much of the bungalow as I could. I had pre-planned everything correctly. The guests list included everyone in my life. Most of whom were dressed as Disney characters themselves. Funniest being Rahil dressed as Aladdin with his magic carpet and Jay as Mufasa whom I confused for Simba from the Lion King, another favourite Disney movie I could watch innumerable times. Mom dressed as Belle from Beauty and the Beast while Kiara was little Red Riding Hood. Arpit, dressed as Winnie the Pooh was a great delight. His big fat tummy was the same as Pooh. But we all thanked God he didn't wear a crop top. Aunt Sara dressed as fairy godmother and was the closest character to real life. The members of the NGO who I worked with were also present along with staff members from Flaunt Affairs.

The party was the most enjoyable day of my life. I had no worries; no tension and I had all the people I loved all together. I ate my favourite food. I danced charmingly throughout the party with my most favourite people.

Mid-way at the party while I was swinging in my green dress from here to there the lights went off suddenly. My home theatre was suddenly bought down and pictures started screening on them.

All my pictures since I was a kid. I was so thrilled that the glass didn't move from my hand. I stood still at one spot looking at the screen. My whole life was put into those pictures. From how fat and ugly I looked in school to my pouting pictures in college. My trips, my friends, family, dad, Flaunt Affairs – everything was put together. Most unexpectedly, by Rehaan. The last few slides were pictures of me and Rehaan, which was a little embarrassing in front of everyone. My hand suddenly fell in his hands as he came out of nowhere and walked me to the screen. I hurriedly put my glass on the table as I walked, praising my presence of mind. We stopped right in front of the screen. Our pictures still running behind us. My legs were turning numb by now.

Rehaan then spoke "Aria, the day you told your mother about your entire life and the things it taught you. I took a video.

I know it's very intimidating but I'm sure you'll be happy with the turn it took. I added everything you have done so far, the NGO, Flaunt Affairs and mixed it with your pictures and achievements. All your bad times and your good. I hope you don't mind that", he giggled. "I decided to put that up on YouTube and named it *The Switch*. Of course because of the major Switch in your life from what you were to what you have become. The video hit 4 million views in four weeks and a lot of people wish to speak to you regarding it. One that I must tell you about is that your favourite writer Aleena, wishes to write a young adult novel on your life".

My hands were all over my mouth in awe by this sentence. I had landed in some other world of happiness not knowing more was to follow.

Rehaan suddenly bend down, right in front of everyone and was on his knee with a mike passed onto him by Jay. Suddenly a ring popped up and before I could think any further Rehaan spoke a few magical words again.

"Aria, I know what you have been through and I know how you are. You underestimate yourself a lot. I want to tell you that you deserve much more. You deserve love and stability. And I want to be the one to do that for you. I want to tell you how special and how beautiful you are every day until I die. I want you to know that I love everything about you. Right from how you actually made me dress up like Eric to how you go out of your way to help people. I want to tell you that you are not perfect, but I'm not either. And even then, I love every flaw in you. I love how moody you are. I love that you openly speak out your mind and are not afraid of standing up for what's right. I love how you take a designer's name in every sentence you speak". The crowd laughed while my eyes filled with tears. "And I love that you secretly have a huge heart. I love you and I want to be able to share my life with you and double our happiness while we divide our sorrows. Together. Forever!"

I was so delighted by the words he said that I felt in my heart a feeling that I had never felt before. I wanted to be able to express or show it but I'd prefer enjoying it quietly while my eyes showed the joy in tears. I looked around, to all the people who loved me, to all the people who were with me at that moment. Their faces glowing as much as mine. The waiting look on their faces I figured was for me to say "Yes" to Rehaan. And I did. I wanted to be with him and I wanted to be his.

"Yes..."

He got up and hugged me tightly. Blood rushed through my entire body at the fastest speed it ever had. It was the most lovable hug anyone had ever given me. I could see the love in his eyes and the happiness on his face.

Suddenly Aleena walked into the hall and I was more than thrilled to see her in front of my eyes. Rehaan contacted her to be here with me on my birthday. She had begun drafting my story for her book. Her birthday present was as good as a present of her coming to meet me. She framed my favourite poem by her and handed it over to me. I could relate to it on point. It read:

As the seeds of sorrow are sown
When the cause of despair is unknown
An ultimate fear arises
Beyond our cure to crisis

As memories sublime and pictures fade
The thought of fall is the same
The sign of pain leads us to fail
When no ship lets us sink or sail

With the tempting roads leading to success
We step forward and build courage
Fall in our way and lift ourselves
To see the bright light ahead of our stay

When assured our way away from astray
We do what we may
Move ahead and not look back
And lead life to have our say.

I got back everything. But at a cost. I had the same things that I had earlier. But this time, I didn't just have friends, I had friendships. I didn't just have a huge bungalow, I had a home. I didn't just have money, I had wealth. I didn't just have an education, I had knowledge and experience. The cost of having everything back taught me that we all are stuck up in this superficial, almost artificial life that we look at from outside. The fake life we see allows us to believe everything is very rosy. And that everything will last forever. We forget that material will evade and looks will fade. What will remain is kindness. The work we leave behind for others to learn from. The effort we take to put a smile on someone's face. The humility we have when we have everything and the simplicity we possess throughout the process. And then it doesn't matter where you come from or how you look. What matters is only who you are and what you do.

Just when I thought everything was over, life gave me a new start. So every time we think it's the end, it's probably just the beginning.

CPSIA information can be obtained at www.ICGtesting.com
Printed in the USA
LVOW08s1330300316

481429LV00005B/90/P